TWO STORIES

TWO YOUNG TEACHERS

DEVASTATING CONSEQUENCES

SHATTERED
PRETENSIONS

COLIN M. ANDREWS

ALSO BY
COLIN A   S

novel
A MATTER OF DEGREE
(Matador, 2011)

poetry & short stories
WHO GIVES A HOOT
(New Generation, 2014)

non-fiction
SHEPHERD OF THE DOWNS
(Worthing Museum, 1979, 1987,
3rd revised edition 2006)

All titles available from author's website
www.bonnygreen.co.uk

Matador
9 Priory Business Park,
Wistow Road, Kibworth Beauchamp,
Leicestershire. LE8 0RX
Tel: 0116 279 2299
Email: books@troubador.co.uk
Web: www.troubador.co.uk/matador
Twitter: @matadorbooks

ISBN 978 1784624 774

British Library Cataloguing in Publication Data.
A catalogue record for this book is available from the British Library.

Printed and bound in the UK by TJ International, Padstow, Cornwall
Typeset in 11pt Aldine401 BT Roman by Troubador Publishing Ltd, Leicester, UK

Matador is an imprint of Troubador Publishing Ltd

SHATTERED PRETENSIONS

comprising

FRAGILE
A short story

A headmaster standing for election to parliament is reluctant to answer allegations in the local press concerning the mysterious disappearance of his wife many years earlier.

OUT OF THIS WORLD

An extended role play exercise creates tensions which reach beyond the classroom, with catastrophic consequences for both teacher and students.

by

COLIN M. ANDREWS

FRAGILE

FRAGILE

PROLOGUE

As usual Bette had risen early to prepare for Sunday School. She would have taken a shower and dressed before attending to Anne-Marie. Clive lay in bed vaguely aware of his daughter chattering away downstairs. He promised himself a few more minutes before rousing Nathan and chivvying him to be ready to leave with his mother and sister.

Glass smashed, the sound unmistakable, the reaction, Clive feared, inevitable. He quickly threw on slacks and a jumper.

He thought the screaming would never stop. Wave after wave from the depth of her lungs pierced the calm of the morning. Her face contorted into furrows, channelling the tears that were already beginning to flow. From the puddle of milk spreading over the tiled floor, Clive could guess what had happened. Outbursts of irrational anger had for years punctuated their marriage but he had learned from bitter experience that neither consolation nor confrontation would do anything but exacerbate the situation. Since the accident in which they had lost their first-born child, the trigger for Bette's hysteria had become all too delicate.

Carefully selecting a newspaper, Clive made to mop up the mess.

"Leave it, damn you!" Bette screamed, "She can clear it up!"

Clive thought he saw light glinting off a sliver of glass in her hand as her arm pointed like a dagger to her daughter cowering beneath the kitchen table.

Despite her temper, Bette had never before threatened the children.

"Enough, Bette, stop it! Please!"

Her head snapped round, her eyes blazing with fury. "You bastard...bastard! You...you dare to tell me? You never...never... NEVER...!" Her voice wound up to another crescendo.

A cup smashed into the wall beside him, scalding him with coffee. Her mother's attention diverted, Anne-Marie scurried out of the kitchen.

His blow, nothing more than a mild slap with the back of his hand, must have caught her off-balance. Still spitting invective, she fell awkwardly, her arm twisted beneath her body. Her screams shrilled – and died. A red stain spread from beneath her blouse, mingling with the white of the milk. The pool of liquid grew larger.

"Mummy? Mummy? What's the matter?" Nathan called in concern from his bedroom.

Clive looked down uncomprehendingly at his wife's body. For one brief moment in his life he was uncertain what to do. A myriad of images crowded his brain, clamouring for attention. Ambulance? The children...they heard the screams...did anyone else?...but if the police were called? Oh God! And Ann-Marie...did she see what happened? Sunday school...what about Sunday school?

"Mummy?" Nathan was coming downstairs.

"Nathan, Mummy's...Mummy's not very well." Clive tried to control his voice and show more calm than he felt. "Please get yourself and Anne-Marie ready." Nathan could cope... would cope, like his father, Clive prayed.

4

"But…if Mummy's ill?"

"Do as I say. Please." Clive thought quickly, "Mrs Webster will take Sunday School. I'll give her a ring."

Anne-Marie whimpered. "Can I see Mummy?"

"Best not disturb her, she's taking a rest now." Clive breathed a sigh of relief as his deception was accepted. He wished it were that simple. "You had better go round to Nan's after church," he added, immediately regretting the suggestion even as he spoke. Nan! Only a stone's throw from the church. It wouldn't be long before she brought the children back home to fuss over her precious daughter. Not that she ever got any thanks from Bette for her trouble.

A knot tightened in Clive's stomach. He felt sick with fear as he reached for the telephone again.

Mrs. Webster, Sunday School leader for nearly thirty years, obliged willingly. On her impending retirement she had herself recommended Bette as her successor, and she still took charge during family holidays.

"Don't you worry, Mr Richards, I'm only too pleased to help. Give my best wishes to Bette. Touch of 'flu is it? There's a lot of it about this year. Would you like me to pop in and…"

"No! Er…thank you, I can manage." Mrs Webster would have prattled on for hours. "Look, I must get the children ready. Goodbye."

From upstairs Clive heard Anne-Marie giggling as Nathan teased and coaxed her into the bathroom. "Ten minutes!" Clive called. He took a deep breath. Ten minutes to do…what first?

Though his own stomach would have rejected food, Clive quickly set out breakfast of cocoa-pops and frosted flakes in the dining room for the children, and closed the door to the kitchen. His wife's body still lay motionless on the floor by the refrigerator. A slight trickle of blood still seeped from beneath her back, which suggested to Clive that no major blood vessel had been severed. He felt for a pulse in her neck, and prayed that he was not imagining the faint response.

Footsteps tumbled down the stairs.

"We're ready," called Nathan.

"Get yourself some breakfast quickly, it's on the table." Clive called from the kitchen

"Is Mummy okay?" Nathan asked with concern.

"No need to worry, just needs to be on her own for a while, I think," Clive answered, with growing confidence that he could control the situation. "Look, it might be best if you stay round at Nan's for the day. I'll let her know you're coming." He paused then popped his head round the door from the kitchen. "I'll come and pick you up later," he added.

"Daddy, can I have some milk, please?"

SEVENTEEN
YEARS LATER

A smart young man in a white tuxedo offered champagne from a silver tray to the guests as they arrived. Probably one of her father's sixth-formers, Anne-Marie thought as she took a glass and made to mingle with the throng already gathered in the school hall. She didn't recognise anybody immediately. Since she had started her degree course over two years ago and Skype had made distant contact so much easier, she rarely made a home visit other than at Christmas. It had been a last-minute decision to attend the reception to launch her father's election campaign.

Anne-Marie eased her way closer to the stage. She was proud of her father, who cut an imposing figure with his athletic frame, clean-shaven face and still, at forty-seven, with a full head of black hair. Definitely more appealing on election posters, she thought, than his main rival, the incumbent MP, Bernard Maidment, an unsavoury old bigot both in appearance and reputation.

The hubbub of chatter died away as Clive Richards mounted the stage, followed by Peta Williamson. Though outwardly they maintained a strictly professional relationship, rumours of a more intimate friendship between them had been spreading in the town since he had declared his intention to stand for parliament. Anne-Marie had quite taken to Peta the first time her father had introduced his secretary to her at a Christmas social. Even then, soon after his appointment as headmaster of the town's largest comprehensive, Anne-Marie had suspected that her father was attracted to the slim and comely divorcee.

"Ladies and gentlemen," Clive was well used to projecting his voice over a few hundred children, "I would like to thank you all for coming this evening and supporting the launch of what I hope will be a long career in politics." He acknowledged the spontaneous applause before continuing. "Now I don't intend to make a long speech on this occasion about my policies as I suspect I would be largely preaching to the converted." He smiled at another short burst of clapping. "There will be plenty of time for that in the next few weeks, and this evening I'd like you to enjoy yourselves – and, of course, the refreshments." Clive paused. "However there is one important item of a personal nature that I would like to share with you. It will be news also to my lovely daughter whom I am so delighted to see here tonight."

Anne-Marie could not help blushing as she unexpectedly found herself in the limelight.

"As some of you will know, I lost Bette, my first wife, when my children were still young." He took Peta by the hand to stand beside him. "Peta has been my rock and guidance over the three years since I became headmaster. She has been a tremendous support to me in my work and, more than that, a great comfort to me in my life. I thought it only right that I should do the decent thing and ask her to marry me. I am pleased to say she is willing to become an MP's wife."

Clive kissed his fiancée, and they left the stage to another round of thunderous applause.

"Well done, Dad, I'm so pleased for you both." Anne-Marie met them at the foot of the steps, and gave them both a hug.

"Lovely surprise to see you too, my pet. You'll be staying overnight of course?"

"Yes, though I've got to get back to Cambridge tomorrow."

"Understood. Okay, see you back at the house later. We've got to shake a few hands here now. You're welcome to join us, you know, family group and all that, but I guess you'd rather be doing your own thing."

"Absolutely!"

Anne-Marie left her father to do the glad-handing and drifted back into the main body of the assembly, hoping to find a familiar face.

"Can I get you another drink?"

"What?" Anne-Marie turned to see a slightly-built young man with shoulder-length black hair, casually dressed in jeans and a zip-up fleece. "Oh, I'm sorry, I didn't mean to be rude…"

"No problem. Another drink? Your glass is empty."

"Oh, er, yes. Thanks."

He returned in a couple of minutes with a flute of champagne and a half pint of beer. "You and I seem to be the only people here under thirty. Are you one of Big Dick's supporters?"

"If you mean my father…"

"Oh, God, I'm sorry…I didn't realise! You're his daughter?"

"Yes. And your connection is?"

"I've just come back to see the old school. Mr Richards has certainly made a difference since he took over. That was his nickname by the way."

Anne-Marie started to turn away but paused.

"Look, I'm sorry for that gaffe. It wasn't the most sensible of introductions I could have made."

"True." Anne-Marie looked at him more sympathetically. "Well, why don't you introduce yourself properly?"

"I'm Tony, Tony Pelotti."

"And you were a pupil here?"

"Yes, for a short while. I don't remember you, though I guess we're similar in age."

"That's because I didn't go to this school."

"Oh really?" Tony sounded surprised. "Look, do you fancy a coffee in town. On me. There's not a lot going to be happening here."

Anne-Marie looked around. Her father was deep in conversation with yet another group of guests. Not a great deal to hold her interest. "Okay. Just a coffee. Don't go getting any big dick ideas of your own." Anne-Marie thought she saw a flash of disappointment in his eyes.

Predictably, for a Saturday evening The Caribbean Coffee Lounge in the High Street was busy, yet still had a few tables free towards the rear.

"So, um…Miss…I'm sorry I don't know your name."

"Anne-Marie."

"That's cool." Tony said in all seriousness. "I know you said you didn't go to your father's school, but how come I haven't seen you around before?"

"When Dad got this job, I was just about to start my last year of A levels, and I didn't want to move at that point. My aunt kindly offered me her spare room."

"Do you still live with her?"

"No, I'm at college, now. This is just a quick visit."

"And where's college?"

"Cambridge."

"Wow, you must be clever! Good looking as well."

"Full marks for trying on the chat-up, Tony."

"Sorry." If he was embarrassed it didn't show. "Tell me, are you excited about your father becoming an MP? I presume you'll vote for him?"

"I'd like to but I'm on the electoral roll in Cambridge. Can't say that I've really thought about whether it would affect my life. Anyway, he's not there yet. Depends on the voters, doesn't it?"

"Indeed it does," Tony agreed. "Has he always had political ambitions?"

Ann-Marie paused before replying. "I'm not sure, really. He's always been very focussed on whatever he decides to do but it's only since he moved back here that he's ever mentioned standing for parliament. I honestly don't know what made him take that decision. Though I know he doesn't have a lot of time for the current member."

"Hmm, interesting," Tony mused, then added, "If it's not too personal a question, how do you feel about your father getting married again?"

"I'm very happy for him. I like Peta, though I can't say I know her that well yet. But then I never really knew my mother."

"Yes, you were young, so your father said. What happened?"

"I don't really know. I was only three years old."

"So you don't really remember anything?"

Anne-Marie knitted her brows in concentration. "I think she was very upset one morning, screaming at dad. She did that sometimes. I don't remember seeing her again."

"What did your father say?"

"He told us that mummy still loved us very much but she had to go away. He also said that she might not be back for a long time."

"I'm so sorry. That must have been really distressing for you."

11

"Yes it was, I suppose, though probably even more so for Dad and my Nan, her mother."

"How on earth did he cope with bringing up a family on his own?"

"He had help from Nan until he got a head of faculty post and we had to move. We went to live near his sister, my Aunty Joan, so she looked after us quite a lot. Dad was wonderful, though. He was always with us whenever possible though he sometimes had to go away at weekends, to conferences I suppose." Anne-Marie cradled the almost empty coffee cup in her hands. "My brother, too, he's older than me. He was always protective of his little sister," she said, wistfully.

"I'm surprised he wasn't at the reception."

"Nathan? He's working overseas as a mining consultant. We don't get to see much of him these days, unfortunately."

"Another coffee?"

"No, thanks. I ought to be going."

"Can we meet again? If you'd like to."

"As I've said, Tony, I'm not back here very often. And you haven't told me much about yourself."

"Not a lot to tell, really. Local lad, working class background." Tony pulled out a diary from his pocket. "Look, have you got an email so we can keep in touch? You can always block it as spam."

***

"Come in!" Max Boswell, editor of the Southern Messenger, bellowed, not bothering to look up.

Tony Pelotti sidled in and stood in front of the cluttered desk while his boss finished scribbling.

"Well?" said Max curtly. His impatience with cub reporters was legendary.

"I think I may have an angle on Clive Richards. You asked me to go along to…"

"Don't waste time telling me something I already know! Get on with it."

"It's about what happened to his first wife."

"Left him, didn't she, I seem to recall."

"Well, that's what he would have us believe, but I have a feeling he's got something to hide."

"A feeling?" Max said with heavy sarcasm. "And to what do we owe this feeling?"

"I had a long chat with his daughter. Quite a pretty girl, actually."

"Keep to the point!" Max snorted.

"Well, she was very young, but remembers clearly her mother screaming. And she never saw her again. Didn't even come to her Nan's funeral."

Max leant back in his chair, hands behind his head. "And you think that's suspicious?"

Tony stood his ground. "I think it's worth looking into the circumstances of Mrs Richards' disappearance."

"Hmm." Max stroked his stubbled chin. "Well, if you can find some dirt on Richards then it would help our major shareholder no end. Our Bernard's rather complacent, and I don't think he fully realises the threat that Richards poses to his seat."

Tony allowed himself a brief smile.

"You seeing the girl again?"

"She lives away but I've got her email address."

"Get her into bed and she'll reveal all."

Tony's smile grew wider.

★★★

"Have you seen the Messenger?"

Peta sounded anxious. Her call so early was unexpected, particularly since they'd both be in the office by half past eight.

"Not yet. Why?"

"That bloody reporter again! He's making new insinuations about you and Bette. You need to do something about him or he's going to seriously affect your election chances. People are already beginning to talk."

"Okay, thanks for that. I'll have a look at what he's said." Clive cradled the phone by his ear as he extracted the Southern Messenger from the Guardian folded together on the kitchen table. "We'll talk later. Don't worry, love."

With the local rag effectively controlled by his rival, Bernard Maidment, Clive had not been surprised that the reception at the school had been given only an inside page paragraph in the previous week's edition. Nor had he been unduly concerned that the report had linked his engagement announcement with a mention of Bette's disappearance from his life.

Even from a quick scanning, it was clear to Clive that the new front-page feature would cause some people – perhaps even many people – to question his integrity. With his own campaign photograph next to the block headline, *'What happened to Bette?'* the article was short on facts but rich in innuendo. The message was clear: what has this man got to hide?

During the short drive to school Clive pondered not only on how to respond to the Messenger's piece but also how far to take Peta into his confidence at this stage.

"I must say you seem to be taking this matter very calmly," Peta said at the first real opportunity they had for private conversation, after morning assembly. "Can't you sue the little bastard?"

"I am concerned, naturally," Clive replied, "but Pelotti's been quite careful not to give any grounds for a libel action."

"But what about this claim of Bette screaming just before she disappeared?"

"Anne-Marie's the only person he could possibly have got that from, though how the hell he did so, I've no idea."

"I did see her leaving the reception with a scruffy long-haired youth."

"Oh. That would be Tony Pelotti."

"You know him?"

"Unfortunately yes. I expelled him for bringing drugs on to the premises. Always denied it of course, claimed he'd been set up."

"So he could have it in for you?"

"Probably. Though I did him a favour at the time by not involving the police. Don't expect he sees it that way."

"What are you going to do about him?"

"Well, I'd better warn Anne-Marie about speaking to him again. Though as she's away in Cambridge I don't think that's very likely."

Peta puckered her brow. "Is it true, then, about the screaming?"

Clive nodded.

"What aren't you telling me, Clive? Dammit, I have a right to know, if I'm going to marry you!" Peta flushed, then took his hand. "I'm sorry, I didn't mean to raise my voice."

Clive paused before replying. "Ever since her accident, Bette used to become hysterical if she heard glass breaking. One morning Anne-Marie accidentally knocked a bottle off the kitchen table and it set Bette off."

"And?"

"It's complicated."

"Don't you trust me?"

"Yes, of course I do."

"So why can't you tell me now?"

"I have an idea of how I can turn all this mud-slinging to my advantage in the election but timing is crucial. I'm worried that if I were to share the knowledge of what really happened with you now there is a possibility that under the extreme media pressure we will be subjected to in the coming weeks, you may inadvertently let some vital clue slip out in a well-meaning attempt to defend my honour."

"That is so dammed patronising!" Peta flared again.

Clive looked anxiously towards his office door, fearing that she might be overheard. "Peta, please!" He made to take her hands.

Peta brushed him away. "For Christ's sake, Clive, I'm not one of your damn sixth-formers!"

Clive nodded in acceptance that he would have to give Peta at least some of the story. "Though she was only three years old Anne-Marie would have heard screaming. It would have been the last memory she had of her mother before she disappeared."

"Why? What happened?"

"I…"

Someone knocked on the door of his office. Peta tossed her head in annoyance at the interruption. "Dammit!" She shook her finger at Clive, "I promise you I will be asking you about this again later!"

★★★

Tony spent the morning among the archives of the Southern Messenger. Two articles attracted his attention. The first was a small paragraph from January 1982:

BABY KILLED IN CRASH
9 month old baby, Melanie Richards, was killed when the car driven by her mother was in collision with a glazier's van late Tuesday afternoon. Bette Richards, personal secretary to local entrepreneur Bernard Maidment, was taken to hospital with multiple lacerations Her condition is not thought to be life-threatening. The van driver was uninjured. Police are appealing for witnesses. They believe however that the adverse weather conditions may have contributed to the accident.

The front page from a September issue some twenty-three years later was given over to the appointment of Clive Richards as the new headmaster at the county's largest comprehensive school. It made much of his return from the Midlands to the town where he had begun his teaching career as a young mathematics teacher at the former grammar school. That establishment, along with two secondary moderns, had subsequently been replaced, not without opposition in some quarters, by the present glass and concrete complex sprawling over a former green field site on the outskirts of the town. Educational standards had declined, according to popular local opinion, and much of the petty vandalism had been laid at the door of the school's lackadaisical approach to discipline. Clive Richards had gained a reputation in his previous post for efficient management and zero tolerance towards those who broke the rules. The school governors firmly expected him to turn the school around. Besides which, he was a local man.

It was what Tony didn't find in the archives that intrigued him even more.

***

Peta didn't get the opportunity for any private conversation with Clive during the rest of the school day, or even after the children had departed. Under normal circumstances, when Clive had a staff meeting after school, she would leave the office by five o'clock even if the session was still in progress. If he wanted to meet her later he would ring.

Clive realised as he approached his car that his desire to just spend the rest of the evening in his armchair with a stiff whisky wasn't going to materialise.

"We need to talk," said Peta.

"Could we leave it until tomorrow, love?" he said, faintly hoping she'd agree. "I'm really tired."

"I'm sorry, Clive, but this is too important to put off."

Clive nodded. "Your place?"

"I'm happy with that." Peta gave him a peck of a kiss.

Clive tried to smile but it came out more as a grimace.

"Oh come on, grumpy! Look, I just need you to be honest with me, yes?" She took his arm. "And I'll rustle up some supper."

Peta's flat was a five minute walk from the school. On several occasions they had discussed moving in together in Clive's house, but had mutually agreed that they could do without wagging tongues and the disapproval of those who believed a headmaster should uphold strong moral principles by example. With the Messenger's latest revelations, however, co-habitation seemed to be the least of their concerns.

Aware that Clive might still try to procrastinate and both of them might become fractious, Peta waited until after supper to try to get some answers.

It was Clive however who raised the issue of Bette's disappearance first. "Peta, I do appreciate that I've been asking a lot of you. I will answer your questions honestly and as best I can, but there are some details which I would prefer not to divulge until the time is right."

"And when will that be?" Petra asked suspiciously.

"Before the election, I promise."

"Do you know exactly what happened to Bette?"

"Yes."

"Is she still alive?"

"No."

Peta took a deep breath. "Were you responsible for her death?" She saw Clive flinch. "I'm sorry, Clive, I need to know."

"I didn't kill her, if that's what you mean."

"Have you ever told Anne-Marie and Nathan the truth about what happened?"

"No, not yet."

"Why not, for Christ's sake? Your own children!"

"I felt that the true circumstances would be far more traumatic that letting them believe that their mother had walked out on them." Clive sighed. "It was my decision, my judgement. I may have been wrong. I hope they will understand and forgive me when I tell them the truth."

"You're not really going to tell me any more now, are you?"

"I'd really prefer you not to press me."

"Can you tell me whether you ever saw Bette again before she died?"

"Yes, I did."

From Peta's puckered brow and the conflicting emotions, which her facial expressions showed all too clearly, Clive realised their relationship was at a critical point. "I assure you that everyything I have done has been within the law."

Peta's shoulders sagged. She looked up and held Clive's gaze. "I believe you," she whispered, "but please, I do want to know the full story before our wedding."

★★★

Anne-Marie wasn't at all surprised to receive an email from Tony. That he suggested meeting her again in Cambridge, however, was totally unexpected. A little too much of a coincidence, she thought, that he had felt it necessary to visit an elderly aunt in the area. It would have been easy, of course, to ignore his email or just make up an excuse but curiosity got the better of her. He hadn't exactly been forthcoming about himself on their first meeting.

"Good choice of yours, this pub," said Tony, as he sipped his pint.

"Well I've been told the beer's good and they do reasonable food."

"Which is on me, by the way."

"Thanks." Ann-Marie felt no inclination to object. "How's your aunt, by the way?"

"Sorry? Oh yes, she's okay, bit doddery, but she is getting on a bit."

"Are you staying long?"

"Flying visit, really. Back tomorrow. Got to work again Monday."

"And what do you do?"

Tony took another swig of beer while he considered his reply. He wished he hadn't given her such an easy opening to probe his profession. "I'm a research assistant."

"Really? What's your specialism?"

The arrival of steaming plates of bangers and mash gave him the opportunity to change the topic of conversation. "That looks great! Glad I didn't have a big breakfast. Dig in!"

Anne-Marie reached into her handbag to retrieve her mobile phone and recognised the displayed number of the caller. "You go ahead, Tony, I need to take this."

Her smile at hearing from her father changed to a puzzled expression. "Yes, I did, as a matter of fact. Why?"

The colour drained from her face. Tony looked up at her interjections of "Yes, he did" and "Oh bloody hell!" She was staring at him.

"Here right now!" were her final words. She stood abruptly and gathered her bag.

"Hey, where are you going?"

"You snivelling little bastard!" Her eyes blazed with fury. "That was my father. You disgust me!"

The friendly facade abandoned, Tony rose and came round the table. "Part of my job, love," he sneered. "Don't you want to know what really happened to your mother?"

"I do know and it's none of your bloody business!" she yelled. Heads were turning towards the source of the commotion.

"I don't think your father is the Mr Clean you'd like to believe."

"Liar!" Anne-Marie seized his pint glass, threw the contents in his face and stormed out, other customers quickly moving out of her way.

***

The following week's edition of the Southern Messenger pulled no punches. Next to a photo of Clive and Peta together on stage at the reception, the banner headline shrieked,

'What are they not telling us?'

'Twenty-five years ago Clive's first child, Melanie Richards, was killed in a collision with a glazier's van. Her mother Bette was driving. It is known that Bette Richards subsequently had hysterical outbursts. Taking the blame for Melanie's death could have led to such psychological disorders. Living with a wife in a fragile mental state

would try the patience of a saint, particularly with a young family to bring up. Is Clive Richards a saint? Did his patience finally snap?

His wife suddenly disappeared. He says his wife left him. Did they ever get divorced? He also claims his wife died some years later. Would it come as a surprise that we have found no records of any divorce proceedings between Clive and Bette Richards? Nor have we found any death certificate for Bette Richards.

If Bette Richards is still alive then she must still be married to Clive. He has just announced his engagement to Peta Williamson, his school secretary. How long has their romance been going on?

If Bette Richards is dead, how did she die? Why are there no records of her death?

One thing is clear. Clive Richards is being very economical with the truth. Is there another explanation for his wife's disappearance?

Mr Richards has declined to comment. Why is he not prepared to answer these questions?'

Even before Clive left home the phone had been ringing almost continuously. The national press were sniffing about the story, always eager to satisfy their readers' desire for scandal involving politicians – or even prospective ones. He was relieved to find the hacks weren't already camped outside the school gates.

Peta looked grim-faced as he entered his office, and took his embrace and kiss with obvious reluctance.

"Clive, this is getting beyond a joke! You must do something. I've been answering the phone almost non-stop since I got here – and some of the calls are very unpleasant."

"I'm sorry, love. I did tell you that things would get difficult."

"So when for Christ's sake are you going to stand up for yourself!" Peta slammed her hands onto the desk. "I can't take much more of this! And so far you've still told me practically damn all!"

"Bear with me for another week. I promise you it will all be over then."

"That's less than a week before polling day! At this rate you haven't a hope in hell of being elected."

"Trust me. Please."

"Clive…" She was close to tears. "I don't want to believe those stories about you but…you must give me more idea of what's going on."

Clive slumped into his chair, and sat there, thinking.

"Tell me, or…" She bit her lip. "Or…" She picked up her handbag. "Or I'm leaving now!"

Clive's head snapped up, "Peta, that's not what I…" He paused, then said in conciliation, "I'm sorry, you do have a right to know. I should have told you earlier before this…before this all blew up."

Peta snatched the telephone that had been ringing unanswered during their exchange. "Yes?" she snapped, then forced herself to adopt her normal polite secretarial tone, "I'll see if he's free." She covered the mouthpiece with her hand. "Chairman of Governors," she said, handing Clive the handset.

Clive listened patiently, holding the phone away from his ear while the Chairman ranted on, then replied calmly, "I understand your concern about the good name of the school…"

"No, I am not going to stand down." Clive's voice was firmer in response to another tirade. "You will have my resignation as headmaster only when I have been confirmed as the new member of parliament for this constituency."

"Yes I do!" Clive said in response to the Chairman's mocking incredulity.

The phone practically jumped as soon as the receiver was replaced in its cradle. Clive switched on to speaker mode in an attempt to deal with the pile of items in his in-tray at the same time.

"Andy here, Clive! I've been trying to get hold of you all morning." Clive recognised the voice of his agent, Andrew Fawcett.

"Along with about a hundred others."

"This is no time to be flippant. I take it you've seen the Messenger?"

"I have."

"Clive, we've known each other for several years now. I have to…" Andrew paused, then realised that there was no way he could put the question tactfully. "I have to ask you, directly, is there any truth at all in the allegations?" He paused again then added, "And, please, give me a honest answer."

"I am not a bigamist. My wife is dead, but I did not kill her."

"Then why won't you defend yourself in public or sue the Messenger for libel?"

"I will go public, but at the appropriate time."

"You do realise your votes are going into tail spin according to the latest opinion polls? The local party chairman is going ballistic. Wants to pull the plug on you, distance the party from your candidature."

"Well, he's going to have a problem there, with all the campaign posters distributed and voting papers printed."

"It's you who's got a problem. As things are you'd have more chance of being elected Archbishop of Timbuctoo."

"He surely doesn't believe all the mud-slinging in the papers? It's all conjecture."

"He may not but your average Joe and Jane voter will!" Andrew raised his voice in desperation.

"Would it help your blood pressure if I told you I can show that all the allegations are completely without foundation?"

"It would help even more if you could tell me when!"

"At the live debate next week."

"Bloody hell, you'll be hung, drawn and quartered before then!"

"In the media perhaps. I'll still be here. And I'll win."

His agent paused before replying. "You've got something up your sleeve, haven't you, you sly old bastard? Care to give me a hint?"

"No."

"Well, I hope your high-risk strategy pays off. Otherwise we're both out of a job."

"Trust me."

As soon as Clive had terminated the call Peta started to speak then changed her mind. Her eyes were red and moist.

"I'm sorry, Peta. I know it's difficult for you. Tonight, I promise you will have the full story." She buried her face in her hands. "And I know I'm asking others to keep faith with me. Any other calls you get please just take their name and tell them that I am unavailable to comment at the moment."

Peta nodded.

The atmosphere in the staff meeting after school was tense. Clive kept the agenda and discussions as brief and businesslike as possible, well aware that one or two teachers would welcome the opportunity to embarrass him by raising the newspaper allegations. And once the subject had been broached several others would follow like sheep.

Clive realised that the media witch hunt was about to gather pace when he had to weave around several unfamiliar cars to get into his drive. He was surrounded by reporters before he'd even got out of the car. He pushed his way through them to his front door with a terse "No comment" to the barrage of barbed questions which hit him like pellets from a shotgun; "Where is Bette?" "Are you going to resign?" How long have you been sleeping with your secretary?" "Did you kill your wife?" And more.

He needed a stiff whiskey. He ignored the door bell ringing as he poured out two fingers from the decanter. The bell rang again, longer this time, followed by a tap on the window. A man in a suit held some kind of identity card to the pane. Clive put the glass down. "Bloody parasites!" he muttered.

"Mr Richards?" the taller of the two men said, unnecessarily, "I'm Detective Inspector Cooper, and this is my colleague Detective Sergeant Wilson. May we have a word with you?"

"Come in." Clive said, but not before at least one flash from the cameras focussed on his door. He was not surprised to get a call from the police.

"You will be aware, of course, of the various allegations that have been made against you in the newspapers," D.I. Cooper began. "Following on certain information which we have received, we are obliged to look into, ah, shall we say, unexplained issues regarding your wife's disappearance."

"I understand."

"Would you care to give us your own recollection of the events?"

Clive spoke for nearly twenty minutes, with only a brief interjection from the inspector for clarification on one detail. The sergeant's face showed increasing scepticism about what he was hearing but his superior, whilst probably intrigued by Clive's account, listened impassively.

"That's put a very different complexion on the matter, if what you say is true. You appreciate that we will have to verify the detail. I'd like to you come down to the station to make an official statement."

"No problem. I would like to have my solicitor present, however."

"That won't be necessary. We are not talking about a statement under caution."

"Nevertheless, I must insist. I have another matter which I wish to bring to your attention."

The inspector's eyebrows registered surprise. "Really? And that is?"

"Later," said Clive.

A pile of unopened letters grew larger by the day on Clive's desk and most of his emails he sent unopened to the recycling bin. Nor were his critics confined to posting derogatory and disgusting comments on the social media sites. Parents at the school gate became openly hostile in their attitude, some even resorting to colourful verbal abuse. His staff carried out his instructions with defiant bad grace.

Peta stood by him, coping with the isolation of her fiancé as best she could at work but reluctant to be seen in public with him otherwise. She could not face being the target of invective whether directed at Clive or sometimes at herself.

The last edition of the Messenger was no less inflammatory. '*Clive Richards is now helping police with their enquiries,*' it proclaimed and displayed photographs of the detectives at his home and of entering the police station with his solicitor. In case anyone was still ignorant of the issue, all the details and innuendo were regurgitated, with calls for his sacking and prosecution.

It took a great deal for the three of them, heads held high, to run the gauntlet of the baying crowd. Police had to clear shouting people from the entrance to the town hall. An egg clearly intended for Clive shattered on the uniform of a security guard.

The hall was packed, the audience eagerly anticipating the public crucifixion of one candidate's reputation and political aspirations. Jeers and catcalls greeted Clive as he took his seat on stage. The applause was loudest for Bernard Maidment, with modest acclaim for both the woman standing for the Liberal Democrats and the UKIP no-hoper.

The only female candidate had seen a surge in support in the opinion polls, almost entirely at Clive's expense, but what she had to say was clearly regarded as the warm-up to the main event.

Bernard began his speech surprisingly gently, reminding the electorate of his impressive record (his words) over the past four parliaments, and his loyal support for the good work of the recent government. He cleared his throat. The audience fell silent.

"Ladies and gentlemen, I am a passionate supporter of our democracy. Although I am honoured by the support you have given me over the years, I always welcome the opportunity to defend my record against worthy opponents. Do I have worthy opponents? Though I may not agree with their policies I have no reasons to doubt that candidates from the Lib Dems and UKIP are honourable people." Bernard bowed towards them. "But can I say the same of Clive Richards?"

"No!" came the yell from the audience.

Bernard raised his hands to call for silence. "You have seen the allegations concerning the disappearance of his wife many years ago. I do not intend repeating them here. But I ask you, would you put your trust in a man who has declined every opportunity to explain what happened to her? Perhaps he is reluctant to do so lest he should break God's commandment, 'Thou shall not lie!'"

The audience laughed politely, as Bernard intended.

"But how many of the Lord's other commandments has he broken?" Is he a worthy opponent? I think not."

Bernard sat down to a massive burst of applause. Many of the audience gave him a standing ovation.

When Clive rose to address the assembly it took several minutes for the Chairman's appeal for silence to be accepted.

If the public were expecting Clive to look flustered or troubled in any way by the proceedings they were disappointed.

"Ladies and gentlemen, I would like to talk to you about what I hope to do for you, the people of this constituency, if I am elected…"

"No chance of that, you bastard," yelled a bearded gent standing up from the middle of the audience. Stewards moved towards him.

"…but first I must respond to the personal attacks on my character. I have been accused of being an adulterer, a bigamist and perhaps a murderer. I am none of these."

Jeers came not only from the bearded gent, being manhandled out of the room, but by many others in the audience.

"On the contrary I wonder why the Messenger has not seen fit to mention the affair of its majority shareholder with my late wife…"

"That's a lie!" Maidment shot to his feet.

Clive waived some papers extracted from a folder. "I have evidence of the honourable Bernard Maidment's relationship with Bette Richards." He made honourable sound like a term of abuse. "I also have irrefutable proof of financial irregularities involving Maidment Construction in the building of our new school. I have placed this information in the hands of the police."

Bernard Maidment, his face as red as a beetroot, lunged

towards Clive. His agent restrained him, mouthing, "Sit down, you fool."

After a brief moment of silence as the assembly took in the revelations, the hall erupted in bedlam as everyone tried to talk at once and the bank of reporters from the press tapped furiously on their smart phones. The television cameras seemed uncertain as to where to focus next.

When the meeting had once more been brought to order, the Chairman motioned to Clive to continue.

"I will admit to deceit..."

"Ha!" his opponent interjected, hoping to salvage some dignity.

"...but I hope you will understand the reason when I have presented the facts to you. All, incidentally, fully verifiable by any half-competent investigator." Clive fixed his eye on Tony Pelotti at the press table.

"When my daughter was only three years old, my wife suffered a tragic accident at home. She dropped a milk bottle in the kitchen, fell, and was injured. She was taken to A & E where I was told that shards of glass had severed her spinal chord and she had suffered irreversible brain damage. In short, she was likely to remain in a vegetative state for the rest of her life. I arranged for her to be cared for in a nursing home where she was admitted under her maiden name. I can give you the name of the home. It's not local. Although she never ever gave any indication of recognising me, I visited her regularly over the years until she died, six years ago."

Clive took another drink of water. The hall had fallen silent.

"And now to the deception. I could not bear my children to see their mother in that state, and I believed that Bette's mother would never survive the shock, even though the affection wasn't mutual. I gave the impression that my wife had left me. Those who knew us were aware that she had recurrent mental problems following the death of our first child in a road accident. My children and mother-in-law were naturally upset but I think they always held on to the thought that one day she might return. After my mother-in-law died, and Bette did not attend the funeral, I did nothing to correct the impression my children had that their mother also was no longer alive. In fact, Bette died the following year."

Clive looked down at Ann-Marie, quietly sobbing in the front row. "I'm sorry, my sweetheart, I'm really sorry. It never seemed the right time to tell you." Clive sat down, and dabbed at his eyes. "Please forgive me." he said, his voice quaking.

Ann-Marie nodded gently.

17 YEARS EARLIER

I had just enough time. Time to run Anne-Marie and Nathan to their Nan's house. But no time to stop and chat. I knew the ambulance would have to take a significant diversion around a road closure due to a burst water main. I was thankful its route would also draw far less attention as it would approach our house at the edge of the town through open fields.

I didn't try to move Bette. I wanted the paramedics to see for themselves how the accident had occurred. I took her pulse again. Still there – but very faint.

I followed the ambulance to the new A & E unit at the county hospital by car. One of the paramedics had done his best to reassure me that everything was going to be all right but his colleague had looked very worried.

Then the bombshell. During the three hours I'd been waiting for news I had prepared myself for the possibility that Bette might not make it, and even how I would have to tell the children that their mother wasn't coming home. But what the grim-faced consultant told me was in many respects far worse. She was going to need constant care and as for her quality of life, it would be virtually non-existent.

It would have been better if she had died. I loved Bette but her fragile mental state had been putting a strain on our marriage. And after the latest incident I would always have had some apprehension about her behaviour with the children in future hysterical outbursts. That there would have been such events, I had no doubt.

After I'd seen her in the hospital bed, a myriad of drips and wires attached to her immobile, unresponsive body, I was told that it would be extremely unlikely that she would ever recognise me. If there had been the possibility of turning off a life support machine I might well have consented but that wasn't an option I was given.

I knew I could not bear to let Anne-Marie and Nathan or indeed her own mother see her in such a state. The solution came to me as I was thinking about how to cope with Bette's needs in the long term, as it was virtually certain that the hospital would be able to accommodate her only for a limited time.

My older sister, Joan, held a position of responsibility as administrator at a private nursing home in the Midlands. If I could get Bette transferred there, I knew she would be in good hands. Money would not be a problem since we'd made very good investments with the considerable sum Bette had eventually received from the van driver's insurance company.

I felt that Bette's mother would not find it too difficult to believe that her daughter had left me, at least temporarily. On balance I thought that the children might come to terms with her absence in this scenario rather than knowing that she was so severely injured. It would, of course, require my sister's complicity in the deception, but, living on her own after divorce from a childless marriage, I was sure I could secure her agreement.

Fortunately I had driven to the hospital in Bette's car, mine having been very low on petrol. I drove it a few miles further to our regional airport and left it in the long-term car park. It was one of those where one took a ticket on entry and then paid the required fee on exit. It was likely it would be there for weeks before anyone checked. I destroyed the ticket. I got back home by public transport late in the afternoon.

ONE MONTH AFTER THE ELECTION

"Will you be moving to London, Dad?"

Clive patted his new wife's arm and raised his wine glass to his daughter and son, "This is our family home. Though I suppose I'll have to get a flat, somewhere handy for Westminster."

"Tell me, do you really have proof that Maidment was having an affair with Mum?"

"What do you think?" Clive said, in a tone which left no room for doubt.

OUT OF THIS WORLD

MISSION CONTROL 1

In retrospect I should not have allowed their spaceship to crash near to the Omegan territory. I had made the decision, however, that I would intervene in the colonisation process as little as possible. It was my intention to allow the young pioneers the opportunity to take responsibility for their life in an unfamiliar situation and to respond to the challenges with which they were presented.

PIONEERS 1: BRIEFING

Merton Stoke Community College was unremarkable, yet in many ways typical of a small town school that had expanded to cater for changes in government education policy and the rash of new housing developments. It had begun life as a secondary modern to serve the less academic children of the small market town and a large rural catchment area. The brighter youngsters had been required to make the daily thirty mile round trip by bus to the nearest grammar school. In the early seventies that had all changed. The Labour controlled county council actively encouraged the transformation of Merton Stoke's school into a comprehensive for the 11 to 16 year olds. The old tennis courts were replaced by a couple of hastily assembled two-storey blocks, one for science and one for the humanities, to cope with the increased in-take, which was also swelled by the raising of the school-leaving age to sixteen.

After thirty years or so those new buildings were looking decidedly shabby. With the recent experimental establishment of a small sixth form that would give a further rise in student numbers, there was now talk of demolition. A modern three-storey building would be replacing them, as well as several 'temporary' huts that had encroached on the playing fields.

The one session in the week when the year 10 students were together as a registration group rather than following their various GCSE options was timetabled as 'Current Affairs'. Formerly it had been known as PSM – officially Personal, Social & Moral Education but quickly dubbed Personal Sado-Masochism by the students who had been obliged to endure a tedious programme of social awareness twaddle and meaningless group bonding workshops, all intended to make them better citizens.

The students of 10Fleming had low expectations that the renaming would produce anything different. There was a definite buzz in the air, however, as they streamed out of Martyn Carberry's classroom. The young geography teacher had lived up to his reputation for delivering lessons that were often unconventional and always thought provoking.

"Carbunkle's really gone off his trolley this time," Darren Rooney commented dismissively to his cronies as they pushed their way through the mass of bodies in the corridor.

"Yeah, why for Christ's sake would we want to go on a bloody spaceship?" Steve Tancock followed on the heels of his beefy friend like a faithful hound, always backing up whatever Darren said. His thin pinched face and close set black eyebrows gave him a mean and disagreeable appearance.

"To get you lot out of his hair?" said Roger Simpson, who'd overheard the exchange.

"You shut your bloody gob!" Darren snarled.

Roger ignored him.

"I wouldn't mind," piped up an obese, vertically challenged kid with a pudding-bowl hair cut. " Be great…"

"Doubt if they'd find a spacesuit to fit you, Sim," Darren cut him off curtly.

"Yeah, and you'd probably spew your guts out like you did on the big dipper," Tom Anson, the fourth member of Darren's gang, was equally sarcastic. Lean and lanky, with a prominent Adam's apple that bobbed up and down as he spoke, he was in every way the antithesis of Simeon.

If Simeon was discouraged by the remarks of his companions, he didn't show it. "But wouldn't it be marvellous to see all those…"

"You've been watching too much Voyager and all that crap," said Steve, not giving Simeon the chance to even identify his visions.

"Yeah, can you imagine Sim boldly going where no-one has ever gone before?" said Darren. "Anyway no-one here is going anywhere off this planet anytime soon, whatever Carbunkle thinks."

"Except in his dreams," Steve jerked his thumb at Simeon, who slouched behind them, his space bubble of enthusiasm punctured.

"God, Patsy, why did you have to invite her?" Tina Wilson whispered as they sat down on the only vacant bench seat. Her body had begun its change from child to young woman some years earlier, and, though only a month past her fifteenth birthday, she enjoyed the effect her appearance had on older lads. Her image was unlikely to be enhanced by the company of a plain, barely pubescent girl with untidy, mousy hair.

Lizzie Humphrey had spotted the pair and was obviously making her way across the playground to join them.

"She'll be okay, Tinny." said Patsy.

"She's a total wimp!"

"But it's not exactly if she's got a lot of friends, apart from Nikki."

"That's only because they travel on the same bus. Anyway, you didn't ask Nikki."

"She's away today, in case you hadn't noticed."

"But…"

"Honestly, Tinny, what did you expect me to do? Send Nikki a text during the lesson?"

"S'ppose not," Tina conceded.

"Anyway, we didn't really have much choice, did we? Unless, of course, you'd have preferred Simeon?"

"Ugh! That fat slug? No thanks!"

"Bit far fetched, don't you think?" Sharon Tomkins said to no one in particular in the group of her classmates seated around the dining hall table. She brushed the lock of blonde hair from her face, uselessly, for the umpteenth time.

"Why's that, Shar?" asked Jo Pugsley, tall, slender and dark, in contrast to her friend.

"Well…it is, isn't it?"

"Not really, Richard Branson's planning commercial space flights already." Roger Simpson's contribution was as usual pragmatic and factual. Academically gifted, he had a natural air of quiet authority and, as captain of the school's under-16s rugby team, he was a model of physical fitness.

"Thought he was into balloons," said Bram Herbert. His carefully gelled spikes of red hair rising from an otherwise shaven skull looked like a giant coxcomb. It served quite effectively, for those who did not know his gentle nature, to ward off potential aggressors.

"He's been there, done that. Got his eye on the future," Roger came back.

"Makes you wonder, though, doesn't it?" said Sharon.

"What about?" Bram asked.

"Well, they were landing men on the moon back in my grandma's day, and they haven't got any further since."

"No day trips to the moon, you mean?"

Sharon tossed her head dismissively at Jo's remark. "I mean, you'd think that in over forty odd years they would have got further than shuttling men up to a piddling little space station."

"Perhaps Carbunkle sees us as the real astronauts of the future." said Roger.

LIZZIE'S DIARY 1

I'm so happy. Patsy Clements has chosen me to join her crew! I'm going to be the Navigator on her spaceship. And my friend Nikki will be there too.

Of course, it's not a real spaceship. It's Mr Carberry's idea. I really like him. His lessons are never boring – not like some other teachers I could mention. He's told us to prepare for a long journey – not too long, I hope. I want to be back in time to go to Blackpool again this summer.

We're supposed to call him Mission Controller. I'm not sure I can get used to that, but I'll try. I wonder if he'll be sitting at his desk with lots of flashing lights and buttons and computer screens. Perhaps we'll all have to wear spacesuits.

I'm so happy.

SPACETALK

Tina Wilson@cando
@nikotinegirl U ok? Cbk spacewalk nxt wk

Nikki Ridley@nikotinegirl
@cando Wha?

Tina Wilson@cando
@nikotinegirl U me Pats + sorry mouse we r in2 space. C u bfn

MISSION CONTROL 2

What did I have in mind in setting up this whole scenario? I'd been given pretty much a free hand in what I did during the Current Affairs periods, as long as I could justify its relevance to modern life. Well, initially, my intention was to get my students to think about the natural resources of the Earth, and how to make the best use of them. After all, almost every day we can see reports of the fluctuating price of oil, worldwide shortages as more and more nations compete for limited supplies, not to mention global warming, drought, famine and the problem of waste disposal or recycling.

Of course, I could by no means take for granted that the youngsters would respond to yet another environmental awareness project on the 'we must act now before it's too late' theme, so beloved of the Green lobbyists. Even though some kids might harbour a glimmer of awareness that their well-being might be affected in some way, they tended to regard the future as having as much relevance to them as life in ancient Rome. Something to worry about later, perhaps. They're more concerned with the latest soaps, electronic games and tweeting about their social life!

Electronic games? Okay, they would happily spend hours avoiding a grotesque fate for their avatars in alien worlds, and watching the latest Dr Who adventure or TV reruns of Star Wars and Voyager. So could I tap into their enthusiasm for fantasy, space adventure and time travel? If they were on a spaceship they would have to ensure that they had a continuous supply of food, fuel, air and water in order to survive. Perhaps even prepare for a journey of a lifetime to a distant Earth-like planet.

Concerned about whether street-wise fifteen year olds would be capable of remaining 'in-role' for a sustained period, I sounded out my drama colleague and close friend, Bob Hawkins. He gave my embryonic idea his enthusiastic endorsement. Thus encouraged, I sketched out a few ideas towards the end of the summer term and began to flesh them out. I also need enlisted the help of a couple of my scientific colleagues on the more technical points of energy generation and the chemical aspects of waste recycling.

My original intention was for the whole exercise to be one of co-operation, with the different crews coming up with their own solutions but sharing their ideas. I also planned to encourage the students to go on-line to research or follow up the various issues which would arise.

When I first introduced the project, and asked the group to prepare themselves for a voyage of a lifetime, they had been mildly intrigued in the disinterestedly sort of way that only young teenagers can express. I hoped, however, that they would be capable of relating the experiences gained from my virtual world to real life situations. One could say they did this with a vengeance.

It had seemed a sensible idea to allow my group of thirty-two conscripts to sort themselves out into the eight crews I required. I could have opted at the outset to go with four spaceships with a crew of eight, but I wanted everyone to feel they had to play an essential role. There was to be no room for passengers, and I also thought that a degree of competition in being the first to land on one of the four chosen sites would encourage all involved to take their preparations seriously.

Not surprisingly, the eight crews were by and large composed of natural friendship groupings. Only the crews of Darren Rooney and Patsy Clements were single sex. Darren was intelligent and charismatic. The leadership role would have fallen naturally to him but he also had a reputation as a bully with a short temper, and was inclined to ride roughshod over anyone who opposed his ideas. Darren had gathered his cronies about him, all nice enough lads individually but, apart from Tom Anson, with little strength of character or wit to think for themselves. Patsy was a lovely, popular, kind-hearted girl, but quite retiring. Though perhaps I shouldn't declare it, she was also very attractive, petite, with warm brown eyes, long brown hair framing her face, with its freckled snub of a nose and square chin. She was the only one willing to take into her crew Lizzie Humphrey, who was as quiet as a mouse – mousy in appearance, too – and had no obvious friends.

PIONEERS 2: PREPARATION

Nikki waited for the school bus outside her home in Fisherspond, a small village some three miles from Merton Stoke. As it pulled up, she groaned when she saw Lizzie already bobbing up from her seat and waving a blue peaked cap at her. Although Lizzie actually lived closer to the school, the tortuous route required to collect all the students from outlying farms and villages meant that Lizzie was one of the first to be picked up.

Nikki tolerated Lizzie up to a point, but her babble of trivial inconsequentialities, often about her pet rabbit, could be very trying.

And this morning Lizzie was effervescent. "We're going on a spaceship, Nikki!" she enthused.

"Yeah, I heard." said Nikki non-commitedly. "Tina told me."

"Aren't you excited? I am!"

"Not really."

"Oh!" Lizzie frowned, "Why not?"

"Well, you don't honestly think we're going to do anything else apart from sit on our arse in the clasroom, do you?"

"But...Mr Carberry said..."

"Oh get real, Lizzie!"

Despite their attempt at indifference, there was nevertheless an air of anticipation as the students of tutor group 10Fleming mingled outside Martyn Carberry's room. Apart from the fact that the blinds had been drawn, nothing else had changed when they filed in.

"We now need to start thinking more seriously about this space journey," said Carberry when he'd got their attention. "I've prepared some briefing cards for you. And, as you'll have your own computer terminal, each crew has got its own password for access to the programme. You might like to think about designing your own logo based on that code. Now, any questions before we start?"

"How long is this journey supposed to last?" asked Sharon.

"Does it matter?"

"Well, sir, it will make a difference to what we need to take with us."

"Good thinking, Sharon."

"So how long?"

"Assume the journey will last a lifetime."

Several audible gasps came from the assembly. Some frowned or knitted their brows as they took in the implications. Darren looked bored.

"Where are we going?" Simeon squeaked.

"I'd rather not say at this stage. You will find out in due course."

"Stupid pratt," Darren muttered.

"Carbunkle's given us the wrong code!"

"What do you mean, Steve?" asked Tom, who was doodling on a loose page torn from an exercise book.

"Obvious. TWLNR – Tina Wilson loves Nikki Ridley!"

Steve broadcast his solution to the code in a far from sotto voce.

Darren Rooney guffawed loudly, causing several heads to turn in his direction and earning a reproachful glare from Mission Control.

"Ignore the pillocks," whispered Patsy to Nikki and Tina, who'd heard the exchange and were rising from their seats to respond. "They're not worth the effort."

"But what's it really supposed to mean?" Simeon ventured once the spotlight of attention had left the group.

"Who bloody cares?" said Darren, then added menacingly, for Steve's benefit, "And don't get any clever ideas that involve my name!" He glanced at the other briefing cards which each crew had been given. "Right, food and drink. Any suggestions?"

"Few cases of lager. Be bugger all else to do except get pissed."

"I don't think that's quite what Carbunkle had in mind, Tom," said Darren, in a rare serious moment.

"What about cans of corned beef and baked beans, like those explorers…"

"Use your bloody brain, Sim!" Darren interrupted, "Think of the weight! And what do you do with the empties, you idiot! No bloody weekly refuse collection up there!"

"Wouldn't need an engine if we had baked beans," said Steve. "Sim's farts would be more powerful than a rocket."

"Yeah," said Darren, "We could stuff them up his arse!"

"Suppositron power?" said Tom. The others looked at him blankly. They didn't have a pharmacist as a father.

The LWFNR team, captained by Roger Simpson, were making more positive progress in addressing the issues.

"Energy sorted – conventional rocket technology for launch,

then solar panels, with emergency back-up system." Roger ticked the card. "Now, our life support systems."

"The journey may last a very long time, right?" Bram mused. "Therefore…we need to be able to produce our own food… and…"

"Water, too, and oxygen to breathe," Jo contributed.

"What do they do on submarines about air?" asked Sharon.

"I think they have some sort of chemical scrubber to remove the carbon dioxide," Roger replied. "And, of course, they do have a good idea in advance of how long they are going to be at sea. I suppose they could always harpoon a fish if they run out of food," he added light-heartedly.

"Then…" One could almost hear the gears grinding in Bram's brain. "…that means recycling, doesn't it? Like water… and other waste?"

"Ugh!" said Sharon, "That's disgusting! Drinking your own pee?"

"Well, that's what happens here anyway," said Roger. "Water treatment works – the sewage gets cleaned up and clean water is returned to the rivers. At least, in theory."

"And we could use the waste as fertiliser and grow our own food. And photosynthesis!" Jo's face lit up at a spark of a memory from the biology lessons. "Green plants remove carbon dioxide and produce oxygen! Brilliant!"

"Yeah, and we can't have our turds orbiting the universe, can we?" said Bram. "It's bad enough avoiding dog shit on the pavement."

"Ugh!" Sharon repeated. "You're disgusting!"

Nikki had managed to escape from Lizzie's attention at lunchtime for an illicit fag with Tina behind the bike sheds. Like Tina, she was well developed for her age and quite capable of turning the heads of testosterone powered young men.

"Got away from our little mouse, then?"

"Yeah! Christ, she was clinging on to me like Carbunkle's room was the chamber of horrors when we first went in."

"I don't know how you can put up with her."

"Oh, I don't mind, Tinny. Usually, that is, like on the bus journey. I don't think I'd really want to be cooped up with her on a real spaceship, though."

"She's so naïve."

"Yes, but, well, she's not really any trouble, is she."

"Hmm." Tina stubbed out her cigarette and stowed the dog-end back in the packet. No sense in leaving evidence for prowling prefects, a dubious title bestowed on a few selected sixth-formers in return for equally dubious patrol duties.

LIZZIE'S DIARY 2

I was so excited today.

Mr Carberry – sorry, I must call him Mission Controller – got us thinking about our space journey. He had made his room almost feel like a spaceship – all the blinds pulled down so it was quite dark. It felt a bit creepy but Nikki let me hold her hand.

I took a map of the night sky my uncle had found for me but I didn't need it. I'd also borrowed his peaked cap he wears when he goes sailing at the weekend. I thought it would make me look good as Navigator, but Nikki just laughed when I put it on my head in the bus.

We had to make up a badge based on our crew code. Ours was PFSRW – I don't know what it's supposed to mean. And I don't think the other crews knew what theirs meant either. Perhaps it's something the computer chucked out at random.

I don't really understand computers. Mine's very old. I can't do emails or anything like that on it.

Mission Control – there, I've got it right – told us that we would have to work out what to take with us, like food and drink. I don't like eggs. Also, he said, fuel and air. I'd hate to have to wear one of those huge masks divers use, with a great big tank on my back. I did try a snorkel once and I nearly drowned.

Still, I'm really looking forward to next Friday's lesson.

MISSION CONTROL 3

One thing I am quite good at is in writing interactive computer programmes. I've always had an interest in games – board games as a child, and electronic games since my teens. It's a hobby at the moment, although it may be that I'll consider taking it up professionally.

With the benefit of several networked computer terminals and blackout blinds fitted to all the windows, it was quite a simple task to transform my classroom into a spaceship control centre. Not quite NASA perhaps, but impressive enough for young teenagers. They would be able to plot and track the course of their own spaceship on its journey to reach a distant planet I named Terra Nostra. I, as Mission Controller, obviously had oversight of the actions of all of the crews, who nevertheless believed they were fully in control of their destiny. I won't bore you with the details, but suffice to say, I was able to exert some influence on the progress of each crew, introduce hazards such as gamma ray storms, asteroid belts, comets, and so on, and throw in the odd crisis of malfunctioning life support systems. My intention was for those crews who had been less than prudent in provisioning their vessel to suffer the consequences.

The screen view presented to the crews showed a scrolling space map on which the position of all the space ships and various hazards could be seen. In sequence each crew was presented with a scenario and a ten second window to respond to one of five options for action. As soon as a response was given, the options for the next crew would appear, but if no response was given within the time allowed, that crew effectively missed its turn. Obviously the options given to a particular spaceship were not visible to the other crews, only the effect of its decisions.

Without specifically saying so, I'd given the crews the impression that there would be some advantage in being the first to land on Terra Nostra. What I didn't tell them was that only four landing sites were available. Some crews would be rescued from a damaged spaceship during the journey, while others would reach Terra Nostra but be obliged to combine with another crew. Thus, I would engineer the establishment of four separate communities, each consisting of two of the original crews.

To my frustration Darren Rooney proved pretty adept at avoiding most of the traps I had set for him. Rather than be forced to pair up with Roger Simpson's crew as I had intended he was thus able to guide his spaceship to the last available landing site. Even at this stage I could probably have kept Patsy's group away from Darren and his cronies, but I had not reckoned with an unexpected and, frankly, crazy manoeuvre by one of her crew. Without destroying the façade of independent action by the crews there was little I could do.

PIONEERS 3: BLAST OFF

There was genuine excitement amongst the students waiting outside Martyn Carberry's classroom on Friday. The prospect of an hour playing a computer game instead of doing any real work raised more than a glimmer of interest even in the most apathetic young teenager.

The door opened, and the throng made to crush forward.

""Right, steady, you lot!" Carberry's firm voice halted them. "You see I've reorganised the room. Now file in quietly and find the workstation for your crew. And don't touch anything! We don't want anyone blasting into orbit prematurely, do we?"

A few polite chuckles came from the group.

"Cor, what a set up!" Simeon burbled.

"F'Christ's sake, Sim, it's only bloody computers!" said Darren.

"Carbunkle's done a good job though," said Tom.

"S'ppose so," Darren conceded.

Eight tables had been arranged in an arc, facing a large portable screen in front of the whiteboard. Against a backdrop of the night sky the screen displayed all eight spaceships on their launch pad. A further table with another computer terminal and a small anglepoise lamp had been set up at the rear. The glow of the computer screens provided the only other illumination.

"Now before we start our epic journey," Mission Control began, "a short briefing. You will be able to see the progress of your spaceship on this screen. On your own monitor you will have the same image plus other information unique to your crew. You'll have options for action to which you must respond within ten seconds."

Simeon's hand shot up. "Sir, what happens if we don't respond in time?"

"You'll get my boot up your fat arse!" Darren's whisper was clearly audible around the room.

"Darren, that's enough, thank you!" Mission Control then addressed the whole class again, "Well, you won't go up in a puff of smoke, but your spaceship will be temporary immobilised, and that could have serious consequences."

"That means the bloody ship won't move," Darren's aside to Simeon was much quieter this time.

"Oh, and one more thing I forgot to tell you. There are only four safe landing sites on our new planet. The rest of the crews will have to be rescued."

An audible intake of breath from Lizzie.

"Any more questions?"

There were none.

"Okay, I'm giving you a few minutes countdown. You can use the time to discuss strategy if you wish, then prepare to keep your wits about you and guide your ship safely through space. I'll be at the back keeping an eye on you. Bon voyage!"

"Bon fucking voyage to you too," Darren muttered.

"Right, guys, let's make it a team effort," said Roger. "Quick response from each of us to whatever's thrown at us, but keyboard operator makes final decision. I suggest we rotate that job."

"I'm happy to give the keyboard a miss," said Sharon.

"No problem. Jo? Bram?"

"Fine with us." Jo spoke for them both.

"S'not fair! You said I could be navigator." Lizzie was about to burst into tears.

"You couldn't navigate your way down a straight road," said Tina dismissively.

"Hold on, Tinny, this isn't getting us anywhere and we're wasting time," said Patsy. She turned to the whimpering girl. "Look, Lizzie, in a plane a navigator plots the course but it's the captain who operates the controls. That's what I'll be doing, but you'll be helping by tracking our course on the screen. Okay?"

"Aw'right, s'ppose so." Lizzie sniffed, and, consoled by Patsy's gentle tone, added, "Thanks."

Tina tossed her head petulantly.

At first the action was slow, and discussions amongst the crew members fairly muted. One crew failed to act swiftly enough to the computer's instructions and aborted take off. The students caught on quickly, however, and the buzz of urgent advice reflected the obvious excitement as each crew sought to gain an advantage and avoid the hazards. Most responses were completed well within the time allowed. Mission Control ignored the odd indiscretions of language within the groups but suppressed the growing noise levels by flashing up a 'silent procedure' instruction simultaneously on all monitors.

Half way into the exercise, Darren naturally hadn't let anyone else near the keyboard. Tom and Steve just watched the screen and occasionally made a brief comment that Darren acknowledged with a nod. Simeon, however, kept fidgeting and hovering behind Darren's chair.

"You're letting them get away!" he squeaked. "We should be in front, at the top of the screen!"

Darren ignored him. Tom shot Simeon a warning glance.

"But they're nearly all ahead of us!" Simeon persisted.

"Watch!" Darren commanded.

As the space scene scrolled on, two of the spaceships at the leading edge of the screen became engulfed in a meteor storm, and red lights began flashing on their monitors, warning them to abandon ship.

"Looks like we've got to pick up some refugees," said Roger to his crew. "No, sorry, we're okay, there are two other ships nearer."

The personnel from the stricken craft picked up their chairs and moved over to the tables of their rescuers. Mission Control paused the action briefly to allow this to happen with minimum disruption.

Darren and Patsy's spaceships were unaffected.

"Satisfied?" said Darren. "If you can't see where you're going you'll end up in deep shit like that. Now shut up, Sim, and let me concentrate."

Darren was indeed having his work cut out to take evasive action from a comet that streaked across his path and deal with an engine malfunctions reported by the computer. As a result they began to fall behind, fifth of the remaining six ships, two of which were now double-crewed.

"Oh bloody SHIT!" exclaimed Darren, slapping his hand loudly on the table, "Not another fucking balls-up!" He turned and glowered at Carberry, who waved a warning finger. "Bet he's doing it to us on purpose," Darren muttered to his cronies.

Darren's expletive had been heard by all. Patsy turned her head, briefly distracted from her monitor.

"Patsy!" Lizzie yelled, "The time!" She leant over the keyboard, "It's okay I've done it…oh!…oh dear!"

In her eagerness Lizzie's finger accidentally caught the figure 4 key before pressing figure 5. Her entry caused the spaceship not only to drop back but also drift into the edge of a cosmic radiation zone that they had hitherto successfully avoided.

"You stupid cow!" Tina turned on Lizzie, "Now look what you've done, you moron!"

Carberry caught Patsy's eye and motioned, calm down, with his hand.

"I told you it was a mistake to have her in our team," Tina hissed at Patsy. "Bloody pathetic mouse!"

Nikki nodded her head in agreement.

"Stuff it, Tinny, it's only a game. It doesn't really matter. My fault really for losing concentration." said Patsy.

"Hmph!"

Lizzie cowered behind her chair. "Sor…sorry, Patsy," she blubbered, "I was only trying to help."

"Some bloody help!" said Tina.

"Nikki, can you take over from me, please?" Patsy left her seat. "You're not helping matters, Tinny. It was an accident," she said as she put her arm round Lizzie's shoulders.

At the top of the screen a planet, marked 'Terra Nostra' came into view. Four sites, named Delta, Theta, Epsilon and Omega were clearly marked. The two double-crewed ships manoeuvred into position to make a perfect touch down. The next crew in line, perhaps in over-eagerness to beat Roger's ship, misjudged the approach to Epsilon and crashed nearby, allowing Roger to land safely and come to their rescue.

Two ships remained in orbit. Darren only needed to make

the simplest of manoeuvres to take the final landing site at Omega. Carberry grimaced as he realised the implications. With barely a minute remaining before the end of the session it was inevitable that Omega would also be the new home for Patsy's crew.

Once outside, and firmly on planet Earth, Darren's gang gave each other high fives.

"Awesome, Darren, we did it!" said Simeon, eager for attention.

"We?" said Darren.

"Oh, er, I mean, er, you did…"

"Yeah, and don't you bloody forget it!"

"What about the girls?" asked Tom.

"What do you mean?"

"Well, Darren, won't we have to work with them for the rest of Carbunkle's cosmic cock-up?"

"Who said anything about working with them? We rescued them. They work for us."

"They could be our slaves," Steve suggested.

"I like that idea."

"Our sex slaves," Steve added.

"Even better!"

"I wouldn't mind Nikki working for me," said Sim.

"In your dreams, arsehole, we'll save Lizzie for you."

.

LIZZIE'S DIARY 3

They didn't say anything after the lesson but I know they are blaming me. Nikki wouldn't sit next to me on the bus this evening.

We were doing so well. Our ship might have even been the first to land. But I made a mistake and pressed the wrong key. Oh, god, I feel so stupid! I sent our ship into the path of a cosmic ray shower. I didn't feel anything – it didn't hurt, but other ships came past us and we were left still drifting in space.

Mission Control told us we would have to crash land and one of the other crews would rescue us. I suppose we won't be killed – I couldn't live with myself if that happened.

I don't think I'm any good at being an astronaut.

SPACETALK

Tina Wilson@cando
@nikotinegirl @PatClem Need 2 deal with mouse

Nikki Ridley@nikotinegirl
@PatClem @cando What u suggest?

Tina Wilson@cando
@nikotinegirl @PatClem No f use to us Send her back.

Nikki Ridley@nikotinegirl
@PatClem @cando Yeah lets do that. How?

Patsy Clements@PatClem
@nikotinegirl @cando Give her a chance

Tina Wilson@cando
@nikotinegirl @PatClem Why? Better without L

Patsy Clements@PatClem
@nikotinegirl @cando Cbk won't let us. Live with it.

MISSION CONTROL 4

I like to encourage my students to use their imagination, to think creatively and to consider various scenarios that might result from a given set of circumstances. But in allowing such free rein to their thoughts I was perhaps naïve to believe that I could fully anticipate – let alone maintain full control – over the direction that their actions might take.

My design for Terra Nostra was to present totally different environments to the four communities which would be established there. Each group would have the basic resources to sustain life in terms of food, fuel and shelter but in all other respects they would remain isolated from the other three communities for an extended period of time.

Darren's group, Omega, had potentially the most difficult terrain, being a wind-swept, rocky peninsula with little vegetation and wildlife, but with good access to the sea. Unlike Delta, for example, with its flat, fertile, coastal plain, or the volcanic island of Epsilon, the Omegan environment required good co-operation between its occupants to survive and prosper, even more so perhaps than the Thetans in their mountainous, forested landscape.

Freed from conventional rules and supposedly free to organise themselves in whatever way they felt appropriate, my intention was that the eventual debriefing would allow us to explore the various methods of government, from democracy, true communism to dictatorship. I also encouraged the groups to review what, if anything, they would change with respect to their hitherto experience of life on Earth. Furthermore, I expected some lively debate about laws and sanctions against anyone who flouted the laws of the community.

With each community made up of two original spaceship crews forced to come together, I expected some tensions to develop within the groups, but that for mutual survival they would be obliged to co-operate and work together. All within the safety of the classroom, of course.

PIONEERS 4: LANDING

"You'll remember that last week you all survived the journey to Terra Nostra." Carberry noticed a hand go up. "Yes, Tina?"

"We didn't land." she said, then muttered under her breath, "Thanks to you know who."

"Yes, that's correct, but you were very close, and we'll take it that you touched down close to the Omegan site. You'll be joining them."

Tina's brow knitted in thought and then in consternation whispered urgently to Patsy, "That's bloody Rooney's crew! Shit!"

Patsy replied quietly, "I had realised that was going to happen. Not much we can do about it."

"But…"

"Tina Wilson, can I have your attention, please? You'll have plenty of time for discussion shortly."

Tina just held back from mouthing another expletive.

"To all intents and purposes the four landing sites must be thought of, for the time being at least, as totally isolated from each other. A bit like having your own desert island, though you'll find that each site has its own unique features. I've set up some portable display boards to give each group some degree of privacy in this room. Now, you've got forty-five minutes to address the various issues on your briefing sheet before I ask each group to report back."

Darren swaggered over to the Omega designated area furthest from the door, followed by Tom and Steve. Simeon hesitated, looking back to Patsy and her friends who seemed reluctant to move.

"Come on, Sim," Darren called, "and bring the sla…bring the wenches with you."

Sim puffed himself up to look as important as possible, "You've got to come with me," he said to the girls.

"Piss off, you fat freak," Tina snapped, not even bothering to turn her head.

"You can't talk to me like that!" Sim squeaked.

"And why not?"

Simeon put his hand on Nikki's shoulder to get her to move.

"Get your filthy paws off me!" Nikki brushed him aside, "We're coming."

Like a little terrier with sheep, Simeon fussed around the girls as they ambled slowly over to his cronies, and, with theatrical self-importance announced, "Our sex slaves have arrived!"

Lizzie started sobbing. Nikki and Tina, initially taken aback, burst out in a fit of laughter.

"Sex slave? Bugger all use to you, you little slug!" said Nikki.

"He'd be more like the eunuch in a harem," Tina cackled.

"Enough!" Darren flashed an angry look at Sim then said with heavy sarcasm, "Good of you all to join us!"

"What's a eunuch, Steve?" Simeon whispered.

"Guy with no balls. Describes you pretty well."

Patsy hitherto had held back from the exchanges, deep in

thought. "Is that the briefing?" she asked quietly, pointing to the sheet of paper that Darren was holding. "What does it say?"

"Not much to concern you," said Darren. "A bit about what this shit hole landing site is like."

"Which is?"

"Bare rocks and cliffs, and wind."

"And?"

"And what?"

"Well, aren't we supposed to be discussing something, like how we…"

"All done." Darren interrupted brusquely.

"What do you mean? We haven't even seen the paper yet."

"No need. I've decided."

"But that's not fair! We're supposed to work together." Patsy protested.

"You can't do that," Nikki added her voice.

"I can. It says here we decide on process of decision-making. Which I've done."

"Oh, for Christ's sake, you moron, this is twenty-first century England, not the bloody dark ages!"

"Wrong, Tina, we're on some piddling planet in the middle of bugger all."

"But we have a right to have a say in what happens."

"I don't think so. Anyway, it's no different to some countries today is it? Where women don't count."

"Except for sex," Simeon piped up.

"Shut up, Sim!" said Tom. "This is not about sex."

Simeon looked disappointed.

"I still think it's wrong," Patsy said.

"Tough. We were here first. We rescued you. You do what we say."

"Oh, fuck off, Darren!" Tina exploded.

Darren flushed and rose from his chair. "Don't talk to me like that again, you stupid cow!"

"Screw you!"

Darren raised his hand and would have struck Tina, had Tom not restrained him.

"Easy, Darren, Carbunkle's watching us."

In the adjacent Epsilon enclave, Roger Simpson was aware of some early heated exchanges from his neighbours before things quietened down. By contrast, he encouraged a very strong level of cooperation between his crew and the rescued party led by John Brownlaw, who, like Roger, was a keen rugby player. The Epsilonians opted by mutual consent for two joint leaders, Roger and John, to make decisions on their behalf.

Mission Control's debriefing session revealed that the Delta group had gone for a truly communal and democratic approach with everyone having an equal vote in decision-making. For the Thetans, one person, strong-willed Emily Tate, had put herself forward as leader and had been accepted by unanimous acclaim.

Although the majority of students were bussed into school, Tina was one of the thirty percent who lived in Merton Stoke within reasonable walking distance. As was her usual practice she took the footpath through the former council estate rather than the longer route via the town centre.

Darren stepped out of an alleyway and blocked her path. She turned, only to see Simeon and Steve behind her, smirking.

"Well, do you still want me to fuck off?" Darren sneered.

"Preferably. And you other tossers." Tina said defiantly. She was used to standing her ground with her older brother. In her coat pocket her hand felt for the speed dial on her mobile.

Darren pushed her back into the arms of his cronies. "No one tells me to fuck off, you slag."

"Let me go!" She struggled to free herself from Steve's grip.

"What shall we do with her, guys?" Darren laughed.

"She called me a fat freak," said Simeon. "She must be made to apologise."

"In your dreams!" Tina spat on the ground, "Slug."

"You shut up or…I'll…" Simeon shrieked.

"You'll what? Run home and tell mummy?" Tina yelled.

"Yeah," mused Darren, "I think she should apologise…kiss and make up, eh, Sim? Come here!"

Steve grabbed Tina by the back of her neck and forced her head down to Simeon's face. "Kiss him!" Darren commanded, " And then you can kiss my cock!"

Tina brought her knee up sharply into Simeon's crotch. He yelped and doubled up. She then swung her leg back to rake Steve's shin with the heels of her shoe, causing him to release his grip. She turned and ran back up the path while Darren was temporarily obstructed from pursuit by his colleagues, still clutching their injured parts.

LIZZIE'S DIARY 4

I wish, I wish I hadn't been so stupid! It wouldn't have been so bad if any other crew had rescued us, but Darren Rooney – he's horrible. He always wants to get his own way. He won't even listen to suggestions from friends so they just do whatever he tells them. And as for us, he treats us like slaves.

I don't like the way Simeon talks about…I'd better not even say in case my Mum finds out. She says it's not something a good girl should mention.

And it's not very nice where we landed. Mission Control said it's all rocky and windy and cold. Nothing but rough grass and hardly any trees. And steep cliffs and horrible pebbles and seaweed on the beaches. I thought beaches were supposed to be sandy.

What are we supposed to do for food? Eat seaweed? Yuk! I suppose the small furry animals might be rabbits but I couldn't kill and eat one. It would be like killing my pet, Bunkin. Darren insists that us four girls gather all the food and fuel while he and his mates just sit around on their backsides. Patsy tried to protest but he slapped her face. Well, not actually, but he threatened to, out of school, if she disobeyed him again.

I think Mission Control is partly to blame. He told us that we were supposed to decide on a leader, and talk about what rules we should have in our new community. Omegans, we're supposed to call ourselves. I'm sure they were nasty creatures in Dr Who. And what did he expect? No way would Darren have anyone else in charge, and as for rules, well, what he says, goes.

I want to go back home.

SPACETALK

Nikki Ridley@nikotinegirl
@cando U ok? What's with yr phone?

Tina Wilson@cando
@nikotinegirl I'm ok. D + caught me on way home.

Nikki Ridley@nikotinegirl
@cando What happened

Tina Wilson@cando
@nikotinegirl Sore Sim balls sore St shin D pissed off

Nikki Ridley@nikotinegirl
@cando Good 4 U. Report them?

Tina Wilson@cando
@nikotinegirl Not 2 cbk. Keep call

Nikki Ridley@nikotinegirl
@cando No worries. CU

MISSION CONTROL 5

One of the advantages of a simulation exercise is that time can be elastic. While the whole process in the classroom was intended to last just twelve weeks in all, my virtual Terra Nostra world required the passage of many years between certain stages in the communities' evolution.

My next key development was intended to explore the way that people from very different cultures might inter-react when first contact was made. I 'suggested' to each community some ways in which their attitudes and values may have changed over the years, perhaps conditioned by their own unique environment. The Deltans, for example, were to be materialistic, proudly patriotic and self-important, while among the tree-worshipping Thetans, the women took the major decisions and the men covered their faces in public. Those of Epsilon were to be the most outward going and demonstrably friendly, but, because they believed they had everything they needed, they would be offended if offered gifts.

I didn't think that Darren Rooney would have any trouble adopting the Omegan role of jealousy towards strangers, though, given his nature, avoidance of body contact with another individual might prove more difficult.

To prepare for imminent contact with each other I further suggested that each group devise their own way of expressing friendship and peace, distrust and anger, agreement and dissent. The confusion and bewilderment that would inevitably result – even perhaps outright hostility – I intended to defuse and discuss during the post-simulation debriefing.

If only I'd been able to get that far.

PIONEERS 5:
CUSTOMS

Once again the class of 10Fleming milled about expectantly outside Martyn Carberry's room, wondering what was in store for next episode of his space adventure. Tina had been careful to avoid Darren most of the morning but as she joined the waiting crowd he elbowed his way back through the throng.

"This evening," Darren hissed in her ear, "It won't be so easy for you."

"You really scare me," Tina tossed her head. "Piss off."

"Don't say you haven't been warned."

Tina confronted him. "Lay off, Darren. You or your morons touch me again, and I'll make sure everyone hears the phone call."

"What call?"

"I had my mobile switched on all the time you were playing your stupid games."

"You're bluffing!" Darren snapped, though his eyes betrayed some doubt.

"Wanna bet?" Tina pulled out her smart phone from her bag. "And I've taken backup copies."

Before Darren could respond further, the door opened and Mission Control directed everybody to their places in the newly rearranged room. He spent several minutes outlining their new challenge.

"Right, do we want to be conventional or, um, innovative?"

"What do you mean, Roger?" Sharon asked.

"Well, as Epsilionians, we're supposed to have developed our own ways of doing things, like greeting people, and so on."

"Like shaking hands?" said Jo.

"Yeah, and signs for anger and peace."

"Let's keep things simple," one of the rescued group said, "Makes it a darn site easier to remember."

"Okay, suggestions then. Everyone happy with Jo's greeting, just shaking hands?"

All hands went up.

"I guess that's our second point covered as well, showing agreement," said Roger. "What about disagreement?"

"Wagging finger?" Bram said, "or shaking heads?"

"We could use the first for anger," Jo suggested.

"Agreed?" asked Roger. When no-one dissented, he continued, "That just leaves how we would show peace and mean no harm to strangers."

"That's so bloody stupid!" said Nikki as Darren strutted up and down again, one finger under his nose and the other hand held out in a Nazi style salute, "How would anyone take that as a friendly welcome?"

"No one asked your opinion," Steve snapped.

"Yeah, shut your face!" Simeon piped up.

"Get lost, fat arse!"

Darren slumped down in the chair, looking very pleased

with himself, despite his contretemps with Tina. "You got the list, Tom?"

Tom handed him a sheet torn out of an exercise book.

"Right, this is what we're going to do for Carbunkle's fucking aliens," Darren started to make his pronouncements.

Lizzie looked utterly confused by the whole process, and said nothing. Nikki ignored her and whispered urgently to Patsy and Tina, "We can't let him just have his own way all the time, can we, for Christ's sake?"

"Shut up, Nikki, while I'm talking."

Nikki tossed her head and carried on, "What are you going to do, Patsy?"

"I dunno, Tinny, I…"

"I said SHUT UP!" Darren strode round the desk and grabbed Nikki by the hair, who yelped as he pulled her up.

Tina shot up and clawed at Darren's face, "Leave her alone, you fucking moron."

"That's quite enough!" Martyn Carberry intervened, "Now cool it. All of you."

An uneasy truce settled on the Omegan group, Nikki and Tina, glowering at Darren, who curled his lip menacingly.

Carberry cleared his throat. "Now for the next stage, listen carefully." He waited while bottoms finished shuffling on the chairs. "Next week, every group is going to send out delegates…explorers…what you will, to each other group. Two people from a group will visit each of the other three communities. I suggest that different people visit different communities. For the rest of this session, I'd like you to choose who will go where, brief your delegates on what you want them to find out, and, of course, get familiar with your special sign language!" He looked over at the Omegans. "And Darren, remember where you are!"

"Yes, sir," muttered Darren, then added under his breath, "On some god-forsaken fucking planet."

"We're going to be the delegates," said Patsy, firmly but calmly.

"No bloody way!" Darren retorted, "You're not going anywhere! All four of you."

"Darren, I think she has a point," Tom interceded. "If we go you'll be in the minority with the girls. Unless of course you're thinking of leaving Sim in charge."

"I don't mind…"

"Shut up, Sim, I'm thinking." Darren stroked his chin. "You're right, Tom. We need to be strong in our own territory. Can't have the slaves mounting a rebellion, can we?"

"We're not your bloody slaves…" Tina's raised voice brought another warning glance from Carberry.

"We'll keep Patsy," said Darren. "She'll add a bit of glamour and she's not so lippy as the other two."

"You're so…so bloody sexist," said Nikki.

"See what I mean?" said Darren, laughing.

"And what about our little mouse?" said Steve, indicating Lizzie with his thumb. "Do you really trust her to do anything useful?"

"Not really. Who gives a shit anyway?"

"Excuse me, Darren, but aren't we supposed to send different people to different groups?" said Patsy.

"Suggestion only is what Carbunkle said. Nikki and Tina go, you and Lizzie stay."

"That's not fair!"

"So what?"

Tina was pretty sure Darren wouldn't follow up his threat to accost her again. Whatever his shortcomings he certainly wasn't stupid, and he would be far more subtle if he wanted to avenge her challenge to his ego. Nevertheless, she prudently avoided the short cut on the way home.

LIZZIE'S DIARY 5

Mission Control told us we've been on this planet for many years, but that can't be right. We're only five weeks into the term.

Darren is still beastly to my friends but he mostly ignores me, except to tell me off when I break one of his silly rules. Thinks he's God.

Sorry, God, that's being unkind to you.

Nikki was crying when we got on the bus home yesterday. It's not like her at all. She didn't want to tell me but I think Darren was still having a go at her in Maths for laughing at him.

She wasn't really. She only said that Darren looked just like John Cleese playing Hitler in that old TV series, Forty Towers, I think it was. He's got no sense of humour.

I don't really understand what he means by meeting strangers. We've all known each other for years in this class but we were told we needed to be ready for next week. Unless we're having a visit from some funny little green Martians. You never know with Mr Carberry. I hope he doesn't get into trouble if a flying saucer lands on the playground.

I'm glad Darren doesn't want me to visit strangers. My Mum is always warning me not to. She won't even let me go on the internet.

SPACETALK

Tina Wilson@cando
@nikotinegirl No prob with D 2nite safe home

Nikki Ridley@nikotinegirl
@cando Gr8

MISSION CONTROL 6

My good friend and colleague, Bob Hawkins, gave me crucial assistance in organising the first contacts between the different communities. Ideally, I would have liked each community to have had their own separate room, but logistically that was not possible. We split the class in half, so that Theta and Epsilon stayed with me while Omega and Delta went downstairs to Bob's room. Three rounds of exchanging delegates between groups – ten minutes for the visit and ten minutes for reporting back – meant a pretty tight schedule within the 80 minutes double lesson, with a good deal of movement between the two rooms.

Generally it seemed to go well, though Bob mentioned to me that he'd had to intervene when tempers got frayed between Darren and the leader of the Deltan delegation. Almost came to blows, I understand.

I definitely owe Bob a beer for giving up his free period, not to mention the support he's given me since things went pear-shaped.

On the brighter side, I had one of the most enjoyable days in this whole exercise. The antics that the kids got up to in attempting virtually non-verbal inter-group communication with mutually incomprehensible sign language had the whole room – myself included – in fits of laughter.

PIONEERS 6: EXPLORATION

"I'll keep this briefing short," Carberry addressed the class. "We have a lot to get through in the next hour." He cleared his throat. "Your aim is to discover as much as possible about other communities but – and this is important – without verbal communication. Try to keep in role and remember the various signs and customs you have adopted in your group. Any questions?"

"Why aren't we allowed to talk to the visitors?"

"Delegates, Sharon," Carberry corrected. "I'd prefer you to use mime and sign language as far as possible. Imagine you're in a foreign country and you don't know each other's language. Talk only as a last resort to find out about their environment and way of life, not to arrange your weekend social activities."

No other hands went up. "Okay, off you go, then. Delta and Omega downstairs with Mr Hawkins. You've got five minutes before the first exchange."

"Why are they wearing paper hats?" Simeon asked, looking over to where the Deltan group were making their preparations. "Makes them look really stupid."

"You don't need a hat," said Nikki. She turned to Darren and asked sarcastically, "What are your commands, O lord and master? Before we bugger off, that is."

""Bugger off will do fine," said Darren. "Go and take the piss out of someone else."

"Screw you!"

As Nikki flounced past, Patsy caught Tina's elbow as she went to follow. "Just try to find out anything that might be useful, even if Darren's being bloody minded."

Roger welcomed the Omegan delegates with a hug and a handshake from all members of his Epsilonian community.

"Aren't we supposed to avoid body contact," whispered Tina after the third hug and handshake."

"Probably, but what the hell! When in Rome, and all that…"

Introductions over, Roger pointed first to himself then at each of his companions. He held his hands arched over his head before bringing them down by his side. He looked enquiringly at Tina and Nikki, and touched the side of his head.

"I think he's asking whether we've understood," Tina ventured.

"Understood what?"

"His hand signals."

"Dunno. A hat? Shelter?"

Roger nodded vigorously.

"They need shelter? Like they're exposed to the weather?" Tina suggested, "Don't expect Shelter Box operates on Carbunkle's bloody planet."

Roger shook his head, then waved his hands, palms outwards, in front of his body. He pointed to four of his team who stood in a circle facing outwards. They began to make breast-stroke swimming motions with their arms, all moving clockwise until they got back to place. Again Roger looked at the girls and touched his head.

"They obviously like swimming," said Nikki.

"Synchronised swimming?"

"Don't think they'll be entering for the Olympics."

"Swimming all round and round, then?"

A quick nod from Roger.

"Why, for Christ's sake?" said Tina.

Nikki thought for a moment. "All round. All round what?"

"All year round? Hot climate perhaps," Tina mused.

"I know!" Nikki exclaimed. "They live on an island. They were swimming round the island!"

More vigorous nodding from a smiling Roger and hugs all round. He then indicated that it was his guests' turn for charades.

"Where are we supposed to be living?" Tina whispered urgently, "Did God ever tell us?"

"Rocks and cliffs, isn't it? Hang on, I've got an idea." Nikki picked up an imaginary object from the floor, walked to one side, and leant over and peered down. She dropped the object then cupped her hand to her ear as she continued leaning over and looking down.

"High up?" Jo Pugsley suggested.

Nikki nodded.

"Mineshaft?"

Shake. Nikki pretended to climb down using hand and foot holds.

"Mountain?"

Shake. Nicki bent down to gather up something in her arms, threw it away again and held her nose. She next took a few wobbly steps, her arms held out for balance, then demonstrated the breast stroke.

"Seaweed!" someone called out, "You're on a beach with pebbles!"

"And you've just climbed down a cliff!" said Jo.

Nikki beamed with pleasure.

An electronic bleeping interrupted further exploration. "Time up," Carberry called. "Return to your base. You've got five minutes to discuss your findings before the next round of visits."

Carberry's timer evidently wasn't synchronised with that of his colleague downstairs. As Nikki and Tina arrived back Sim was lolloping around the room on all fours while Lizzie giggled. Bram shrugged his shoulders as he left to rejoin his fellow Epsilionians.

"What's Sim supposed to be doing?" Tina asked.

"He's imitating a wild horse," said Patsy. "Apparently we have some in our area."

"Silly ass, more like," said Nikki. "Did Bram get it?"

"Total bloody wanker!" Darren snorted. "Got real shirty when I wouldn't shake his hand then spent five minutes doing this." Darren threw his hands in the air repeatedly and mouthing, "Pouff!"

"An explosion?" Nikki suggested.

"Yeah, whatever," Darren said, dismissively, and turned his attention to his cronies.

"Don't you want to know what we found out?" Tina demanded.

"Not really. But I expect you're going to tell me anyway."

"They live on an island," said Nikki, "and they like swimming."

"Great. And that is supposed to help us, how exactly?" Steve was unimpressed.

"So what did you lot discover, then?"

Steve remained silent. Patsy made a zero sign to Nikki with her finger and thumb.

The arrival of a lad with his head wrapped in white shorts signalled the start of the next exchange of delegates. He was carrying a small tinsel tree. Jo and Sharon and another girl came in behind him.

"Hey, Patsy! Come and join us!"

Patsy carried her cola and packet of crisps over to the bench where Tina and Nikki were sitting. Lizzie hovered in the background, uncertain as to whether the invitation extended to her as well.

"Oh, come on, Mouse, you too!" Nikki called, "S'pose we space freaks should stick together."

"Th…th…thanks," Lizzie stuttered.

"Well, how did you get on as handmaiden to the Almighty?" asked Tina.

Patsy laughed. "Oh, he was being his usual pain. Nearly got chucked out, though."

"Why's that?"

"You know the other group in the room? A couple of their guys with the paper hats came over. They didn't like it when Sim started laughing and Darren said they looked really silly. They fixed him with a stare, pointed their finger at him and began tugging at their left ear. Which made Sim laugh even more. One of them, you know Scott Mulligan?"

Tina and Nikki nodded.

"Well, Scott came up to Darren and almost poked his finger in his face."

"I bet that went down well!"

"Definitely! Darren jumped up and grabbed Scott's hand and swore where he'd stuff his finger. Old Hawkeye had to come over and separate them."

"Awesome!"

"Just as well it didn't happen when the Head popped in earlier," said Patsy. "Anyhow, what about you two?"

"I quite enjoyed it, actually," said Tina. "Emily Tate looked really cool in her long white robe. High priestess of a load of plastic Christmas trees and tossers wearing football shorts over their heads."

"Yeah, we had a bit of a laugh," said Nikki. "'Specially with Roger's lot. I'm in two minds whether to join them."

"What, defect, you mean?" Patsy cried.

"Yeah, why not? You could come to."

"I'm not sure that's a good idea, Nikki. Darren would go ballistic."

"Screw him!"

LIZZIE'S DIARY 6

Today was really weird.

Mr Carberry sent us and another group downstairs to Mr Hawkin's room. He said we had to use sign language with visitors. I can't understand why we weren't supposed to talk to them. It would have been so much easier.

But I don't think Mr Carberry had told the Headmaster. When he visited us in the lesson he was allowed to talk. He got quite annoyed when I waved my arms around.

Bram was really funny. He kept trying to shake the boys' hands but they kept backing away from him and raising their fist. It was such a shame. He was only trying to be friendly. I gave him a hug and Darren told me off.

I don't know who it was because he'd got his face covered. He was carrying a small plastic Christmas tree. His partner… Lindsay I think she's called…knelt on the floor and bowed right over to it, just like some of those Arab people do on TV.

My Mum wouldn't have a plastic tree in the house.

Mr Hawkins nearly sent Darren out of the room for fighting with Scott Mulligan. I don't think it was really his fault because Scott kept pointing at him and pulling his own ear. He had a silly paper hat like a large triangle.

Darren is horrible. He wouldn't take any notice of what

Nikki and Tina said about their visits. But on the bus Nikki told me they'd had great fun in Mr Carberry's room.

I'm worried. She wants to go and join Roger Simpson's group and Tina might go with her.

SPACETALK

Tina Wilson@cando
@nikotinegirl U serious about defecting?

Nikki Ridley@nikotinegirl
@cando B more fun with R than D

Tina Wilson@cando
@nikotinegirl What about Patsy Will u ask her.

Nikki Ridley@nikotinegirl
@cando @PatClem Pats, wanna go 2 R group?

Patsy Clements@PatClem
@nikotinegirl @cando Poss but all or none. 1 more try?

Tina Wilson@cando
@nikotinegirl @PatClem Mouse 2? No way.

Patsy Clements@PatClem
@nikotinegirl @ cando Talk 2moro. Bfn.

MISSION CONTROL 7

I had a problem.

Nikki Ridley wanted to defect from Omega. I probably wouldn't have known about it if Lizzie Humphreys hadn't sidled up to me in the corridor and told me she was worried about her friend. I suspect she was more concerned about how Darren would react. Poor little thing, she takes things so seriously, and begged me not reveal to anyone else that she'd spoken to me.

But it did present me with a dilemma. Should I intervene, perhaps with an arbitrary decision for the whole class that no swapping of groups would be allowed? A quiet word with Nikki perhaps? But it wouldn't have taken a genius to work out that I'd been tipped off and suspicion would undoubtedly fall upon Lizzie. There was also the likelihood that if Nikki changed groups, her friends would follow. Would her new chosen group all be happy with an influx of newcomers? Would it lead to further changes in composition of the communities?

In the whole simulation exercise I'd not given the slightest thought to the possibility of defections or refugees or even a hostage crisis. I was intrigued to see how the situation would develop.

This was certainly a factor in my decision not to take any direct action. Had the situation arisen earlier I might have acted differently, but the next process in the whole exercise required far more interaction between the communities. Indeed, I could envisage a process whereby an individual could legitimately become 'attached' to another group more or less on a permanent basis.

The new development in my simulation exercise involved the 'discovery' in each community of important mineral resources, such as coal, oil, iron ore, etc, in addition to the diverse natural materials already available. Just as on Earth, however, these valuable assets were not evenly distributed across Terra Nostra's locations, and therefore trading of resources between the communities would be encouraged.

I provided some background information on the commercial importance of the various resources and encouraged further research as a homework exercise

I facilitated the establishment of a trade council, at which delegates from each of the four communities would try to negotiate the best deal for their people. Foreign Secretaries were also empowered to visit other communities for direct discussions and form alliances.

I admit the concept was very ambitious, and implied a level of sophistication and intelligence from my students that one may feel is sometimes lacking amongst experienced politicians in the real world. Think about speed-dating applied to diplomacy! Consideration of the issues and problems that arose would, I hoped, give students a better appreciation of the minefield of international relations.

I expected lively debate and was not disappointed.

PIONEERS 7: FIRST TRADING

Yet again, the furniture had been rearranged to facilitate the next stage of the exercise. Each community still had its own territory, separated by moveable display boards, around three sides of the room, but at the front, abutting Carberry's desk, was another table and four chairs. A large cardboard sign placed on it stated 'Trade Council' in bold letters.

"You have all been doing very well so far," Martyn Carberry offered encouragement to the students, "but today you are really going to have your wits about you to work as a team. You will be finding out what resources area available to other communities and negotiate trade deals with them. You will all have specific roles in the exercise, as the briefing sheets will explain."

"Will we still have to use sign language, sir?" asked Bram.

"No, I think we can now assume you all share a common language."

"Where's Darren today?" asked Patsy, as she glanced at the briefing cards she'd just collected.

"Got a bug or something," said Tom. "He'll be back next week, I s'pect,"

"Shame," murmured Nikki.

"Well, that's it," said Steve, "We can't do anything if he's not here."

"Why not?" Tina demanded, "Life doesn't stop just because God's got a runny nose!"

"Yeah, and I suppose we just tell Carbunkle to stuff his planet up his arse this week?" said Nikki.

Steve looked for support to Tom, who just shrugged.

"Get a grip on it, you wimps. If you want to sit and suck your thumbs, fine. We'll take over," said Tina

"You can't do that!" Sim shrieked, rising from his chair.

"Oh shut up, fat boy," Nikki's intention made clear, Sim slumped back before she could push him.

"Look, let's be sensible about this," said Patsy. "You see here that we need a Trade Minister and a Foreign Minister. How about if Nikki and I take on those roles? You two can play at being Prime Minister. According to the briefing, we're supposed to act on your instructions, so you'll still be in charge."

"I suppose…" said Tom.

"What about me?" Simeon squeaked.

"We'll also need some Deputy Trade Ministers," Pasty continued. "Sim, Tina and Lizzie could take it in turns."

Lizzie beamed at hearing her name mentioned in a positive role.

After a couple of minutes in whispered discussion with Steve, with Sim trying in vain to appear involved, Tom looked up. "That's okay with us," he said, and added, "Thanks, Patsy."

"God, this is over my head!" Jo Pugsley scattered the briefing sheets in frustration "Have you any clue, Roger, what the hell we are supposed to be doing?"

"I think so. Carbunkle will dish out cards to each group…"

"What sort of cards?" Sharon interrupted.

"To tell us what natural resources we've discovered."

"Okay, then what?" asked Jo

"We then get tokens which we can exchange with other groups."

"Why would we want to do that?" said Sharon.

"Well, I suppose they will have things we want, and vice versa. Like bartering." Roger paused. "Everybody with me so far?"

Nods of agreement.

"How we do the bartering, that's where it gets a bit complicated."

Jo rolled her eyes.

"One person does the exchanges. That could be your job, Bram, you're good at bargaining. Happy to be Trade Minister?"

"Yeah, I'll give it a go."

"We also need deputies to carry cards and tokens and messages. I think they are going to be very busy. Volunteers?"

Three hands shot up.

"Okay, that's great. May need all of you."

"And the rest of us?" asked Sharon.

"Well, you've elected John and myself as joint leaders, so we'll stay here. We"ll need advisers to discuss our strategy in what we need to exchange. And, we'll need someone to talk to other groups directly about possible co-operation on some things." Roger looked around his group. "Something you could do, Sharon? Fancy being Foreign Minister for Epsilonia?"

"Wouldn't Jo be better?"

"No, Shar, you do it. I'd rather stay here and advise."

"Your attention, please," called Carberry, after giving the

groups a short time for discussion of roles. "We're almost ready to move to the next phase. One person from each group – a deputy trade minister, preferably – please come and collect three resource cards and a resource sheet. The sheet will help you to decide what use to make of each resource and what other things you will need to acquire through bartering with other groups. Trading will begin in about ten minutes."

"Pretty uninteresting discoveries, if you ask me," said Jo.

"Apart from the uranium. That's valuable," said Roger.

"Yeah, but only if you want nuclear power," said Jo.

"Or bombs." Sharon added.

"I'm definitely against nuclear energy of any kind," Jo declared. "We can't use it."

Several other members of the group nodded in agreement.

"What about letting another group have it?" said John. "We could choose who we sold it to and demand a high price. After all, we're going to get bugger all for the salt and the wildlife."

"You did well in there today, Patsy," said Nikki as they sauntered over to their Maths lesson on the opposite side of the school campus.

"Yes, thanks to you and Tinny."

"Showed those morons what to do. They couldn't find their own backside without Darren's help," said Tina. "What actually did we end up with?" she added.

"We kept all our gold. Swapped some of our limestone and coal for iron ore from the Thetans. We need all three to make iron and steel."

"They didn't really need the coal. They could have made charcoal from their trees." said Tina.

"Against their religion. Don't you remember the fuss they made over their Christmas tree last week?"

"Yeah. Crazy."

"Do you think Darren will let you carry on next time if he's back?"

"Dunno, Nikki. I doubt it."

LIZZIE'S DIARY 7

It was so different today without Darren. I wonder if Mr Carberry had him captured by aliens.

We all had to pretend to be important people in Government. Patsy was brilliant. She said I could be a Deputy Trade Minister, and I had to help her. And I was the one who discovered gold. It wasn't real, of course, just some bits of card, but perhaps if they find the real stuff I could make a bracelet.

I didn't really understand what was going on. Patsy was trying to swap some of our cards – not the gold, but coal and some kind of stone for other things and she seemed very happy with what she'd done.

She said that Tom and Steve were in charge but I think she did most of the work.

Nikki and Tina were happier too. We were all happy.

MISSION CONTROL 8

The defection from Omega didn't happen. Mainly due, I'm sure, to the fact that Darren Rooney was absent for the first trading session, and his group actually functioned with a reasonable degree of co-operation and sense of purpose. While I don't wish any harm on the lad, I would have been quite happy for Darren's illness to have lasted another week or so. Unfortunately, it was not to be.

I was asking a lot of my students. Even with the limited number of resources I had already introduced, one could do little more than scratch at the surface of the complex issues involved in global trading. Everything had to be pared down to absolute basics. Given a bit more time for reflection some of the brighter young teenagers might have questioned the impossible logistics of a small group of people building a power station, for example.

Encouraged, however, by the positive way in which the class as a whole entered into the spirit of bartering, I decided to go ahead with the 'discovery' of a few plants that would inevitably be controversial. Although seemingly random, from the student's point of view, I was determined to exercise a fair degree of control over which resources initially became available to each community.

While the drug problem in our school is probably not as serious as in the cities, it would be naive to pretend it doesn't exist. The 'happiness herb' card would, I hoped, enable subsequent discussion of the issues in a non-accusatory way. In a similar way, I hoped that the 'leaf of life' elixir and the 'medical moss', a panacea for all known diseases, would lead to consideration of the effects of longevity on world population, resources and employment.

The biggest gamble, and, in retrospect, a possible misjudgement on my part, was the release of the deadly 'poison plant' resource. I had intended that one community would be affected by a plague of alien locusts, against which the poison plant would then be an effective insecticide. I was aware, however, that it also had the potential for irresponsible use – another issue I hoped to explore in the debriefing. I thought I'd played pretty safe by issuing it to a group whom I knew would act sensibly, but I hadn't factored in human error – almost certainly mine.

PIONEERS 8:
MARKET FORCES

"God's back," Nikki murmured, as Darren swaggered into their form base. Simeon, already sitting at his desk, caught her comment and stared at her.

Tina tossed her head.

"Killed all the daleks, Sim?" Darren said casually.

"I...er," Sim stuttered.

Darren ignored him and high-fived Tom and Steve. "So how was life in Carbunkleland? Are we still on that sodding planet?"

"'Fraid so," said Tom, "Though actually it went quite well."

"I hope you're not suggesting my absence..." Darren glared.

"No, not at all," said Tom, quick to mollify Darren's sensitivities.

"So what did you do?"

"Well, it was mainly about trading, I suppose. Patsy did most of the work."

"What! And whose idea was that?"

"Hers actually," said Steve.

"And you two twats let her walk over you!" Darren's voice was getting louder.

"I didn't want her to…"

"Shut up, Sim! I didn't ask you." Darren snorted, " And what about the other two bitches?"

"No problem. They spent most of the time liaising with the other groups," said Tom, "on our instructions, of course."

"Of course!" Darren said sarcastically, "Well, I'm in charge again now, so they'll do what I say."

"I think it would be better to leave things as they are," Tom said.

"You do, do you? Well, I bloody…"

The babble of chatter died down as their form tutor entered with the register.

Expecting conflict, Patsy was amazed to find Darren in relatively good humour as they settled down at the start of the session in Carberry's room.

"Tom's been telling me that you did a good job last week, so I'm going to let you all continue for the time being at least." Darren paused, amused by the expressions on the girls' faces. "But remember, you don't do anything without my say so."

"Wouldn't dream otherwise," said Nikki, her sarcasm lost on Darren.

"So what have we actually got?" Darren asked.

"We're quite well off, really," said Patsy, " Gold, limestone, coal and some iron ore I got hold of."

"Anyone else got any of those?"

"Gold probably not, the others possibly."

"Good. And what else is out there?"

Patsy looked at Nikki for support before replying. "Not sure, really. Mostly food, fuel and minerals, I think."

"And Mr Carberry's got more cards to hand out." Lizzie chipped in, then blushed for speaking out so boldly.

"Uhuh," Darren acknowledged. "Right, first priority for Nikki and Patsy is to find out what's available.

The Epsilonians were still undecided what to do with their uranium.

"No point in keeping it if we're not going to use it," John Brownlow was adamant.

"The reason we're not using it is because we're against nuclear power," said Jo, "and if we let another group have it, we've no control over what they then do."

"True, but it is only a game," said Roger.

"It's the principle, though," Jo persisted.

"Can we really afford not to use it for bargaining?" said John. "After all, we've got little else of value."

"How about…what if we traded it only with a group we trusted?" Roger suggested.

"Yeah, wouldn't want that idiot Rooney to get his hands on it!" said Sharon.

"I'm still not happy,"

"Look, Jo, I appreciate your concerns, but let's take a vote on it," said Roger, "for trading with a responsible group, that is. Those in favour?"

Four hands went up.

"Against?"

Three hands.

"But you've not voted, Roger!" Bram complained.

"I'm in favour."

Carberry called the class to order once again. "Now you've had a few minutes to remind yourselves where you got to last time and plan your strategy for today, we'll get things under way. You'll have some new discoveries and I may call a suspension of trading at any time if I feel it is necessary for you all to review your progress. All clear?"

The trading session opened tentatively but soon became lively as more resources became available and the students began to realise the value of certain materials in the generation of electricity and 'manufacture' of other important products.

"We need steel," Roger announced. "Jo, tell Bram to get us steel – and sandstone!"

"In exchange for what?" asked Sharon.

"Whatever."

"Anyone for diamonds?" came a call from Lindsay, the Thetan rep at the Trade Council table.

"Why, you giving them away?" said Bram.

"Dream on! What have you got?"

"Shitload of rock salt, going cheap."

"I've got bauxite," said Scott Mulligan from the Deltans.

"What's that?" asked Lindsay.

"Dunno."

"We'll have some," Patsy offered, "It's aluminium ore. If you've got electricity we can make aluminium."

"Have you?" said Bram, as Sharon whispered some instructions in his ear.

"Well, that would be telling, wouldn't it?" said Patsy sweetly, then turned to Scott, " Swap you steel for…"

"Hey! We need that," Bram interrupted.

"And you've got what?" asked Patsy. "You can keep your pinch of salt."

"Fast growing fat furry animals for food and clothes?"

"I don't think so!"

"Uranium?" Bram said, tentatively.

"That'll do!"

"And who's got sandstone?" Bram asked.

Darren studied the latest delivery from Lizzie. "Well this is getting interesting. Seems we've got a tribe of primitive humanoids living in our area."

"What's a humanoid?"

"Sort of human but thick as pig-shit. Bit like you, Sim," said Darren.

"Why do you assume they're stupid?" asked Tom.

"Must be, if they're prepared to work for nothing, as it says here." He flipped the next card over. "Hey, and look here! Happiness herb!"

"Well, you'll know how to deal with that," said Tina, who handed Darren the products of Patsy's trading.

"You mind your own bloody business!" Darren snapped. He glanced briefly at what she'd given him, his eyes registering surprise.

"Too close to the truth?" Tina persisted.

"You shut your mouth!" Darren stood up angrily, scattering the resource cards on the floor.

Steve scooped up the cards and studied each one carefully. His brow furrowed at one in particular. "Darren, look…"

"What, for Christ's sake?" His altercation with Tina had caught the attention of Carberry, who signalled him to calm down. Tina flounced off to join Nikki.

"This card…it's a poison plant?"

"So?"

"It was in with the happiness herb cards. Could be useful."

"Hmm, yeah," Darren mused.

"It's a mistake," said Lizzie, "I was only supposed to have the herbs. I'll take it back."

"No you bloody won't!"

"But…" Lizzie burst into tears.

"Stop snivelling and find out where the rest of this stuff is."

"Why, Darren?" asked Sim.

"We're going to take charge of Carbunkle's poxy planet." Darren turned to Lizzie who hovered behind his chair, wiping her eyes with her sleeve. "You still here, Mouse? Go on, you've got your orders."

"Yes, sod off!" Sim added, knowing that Lizzie wouldn't respond like Tina or Nikki, if at all.

Darren waited until Lizzie had scampered out of earshot. "Right, here's what we're going to do. We've got an army of zombies and we'll have the weapons."

"You mean to attack the others?"

"Sort of, Steve. Not physically but we'll threaten to destroy them if they try to resist our demands."

Tom looked dubious. "Carbunkle won't like it."

"Stuff Carbunkle. Aren't we supposed to control our own lives in his fantasy?"

"Yeah, I suppose, but…"

Carberry chose that moment to call a halt to the proceedings, and asked everyone to return to their base. "We will have time for another short period of trading before the end of this session, but I think it would be useful to review what you have achieved so far and where we are going. Next session will again focus on trading but there will be a few surprise developments in store."

"Yeah, and one you don't know about," Darren whispered to Tom.

"Hopefully we will conclude the simulation in the following week, which will then give us time to evaluate the exercise and discuss the various issues which have arisen."

"Pompous twat," Darren muttered.

"You've got something to say, Darren?" Carberry asked.

"Not important," Darren said. "Sir."

"Five minutes' group discussion then before you resume trading."

"Good job done, Bram, you got us the steel," said John.

"Who did you get it from," asked Roger casually, "in case we need some more."

"Oh, from Patsy."

"What did you give her in exchange?" said Roger.

"Well, she didn't want salt or fur, so I gave her uranium."

"Oh bloody hell!" Jo exclaimed.

"What's wrong?" said Bram.

"You do realise that she's in Darren's group? He's the last person I'd trust with it."

"Well, what was I supposed to do, Jo?" Bram complained. "I was told to get steel and that's the only thing she'd take."

"He's right, Jo," said Roger, "but we're not going to part with any more uranium, whatever."

Lizzie fidgeted, trying to decide whether to say anything or not when Darren had finished giving his instructions.

"Patsy, wherever you got that uranium from, I want more. Use the gold if necessary."

Patsy frowned.

"And I don't suppose our little mouse has found out the source of the poison plant yet?"

Lizzie froze like a rabbit in car headlights.

"Well, that's next on our shopping list."

"Why?" said Tina

"Pest control," sneered Darren.

"Kill off a mouse or two."

"That's not funny, Sim." said Nikki.

LIZZIE'S DIARY 8

I wish it had been like last week.

Darren didn't want Patsy to carry on, but Tom persuaded him to let her and Nikki do the same job. I like Tom. He's nice, and lets me join in with the others. Not like Darren who just pretends I'm not there.

I didn't know I'd been given a horrible poisonous plant. I wouldn't have touched it but it was hidden in some other herbs. I made sure I washed my hands properly after the lesson. I'm sure Mr Carberry shouldn't have given it to me but Darren wouldn't let me take it back. I'm worried that everyone will blame me. He's asked me to get more but I'm not going to do it. I shall take it home with me and burn it.

Mr Carberry told us to be ready for some surprises. I hope they're nice ones.

SPACETALK

Nikki Ridley@nikotinegirl
@cando Mouse got bombs & poisons on brain. Panicked all way home. God!

Tina Wilson@cando
@nikotinegirl So f serious

Nikki Ridley@nikotinegirl
@cando Pissed me off. Told her to cry on cbk shoulder

Tina Wilson@cando
@nikotinegirl Will she?

Nikki Ridley@nikotinegirl
@cando Dunno prob

MISSION CONTROL 9

Just as the various communities were beginning to feel secure, I hoped, in their new environment, and the concept of co-operation across the groups began to develop through exchange of important resources, I planned to throw the odd spanner in the works; a few natural disasters such as earthquake, volcanic eruption and typhoon, together with the odd 'man-made' economic or social crisis. To maintain the impression of fair play, I made sure that every community would face at least one major incident, though some would be potentially far more seriously affected than others.

From Lizzie's comment to me about Darren's plans for WMDs and world domination – the poor girl always took things so seriously – I already had an inkling that he might be planning some mischief. My guess was more or less confirmed by his reaction to the earthquake disaster intended for his community. I hadn't really expected to face a serious challenge myself in the classroom. Asylum seekers I could cope with but a direct accusation of deliberately obstructing a particular group, even if it had a degree of truth, required an unplanned response on my part. I took a gamble that, by shuffling all the 'nasty' cards in full view, my rusty sleight-of-hand skills would still result in Darren making a selection that would be unfavourable.

I had, however, seriously underestimated his anger and frustration. Never before in my teaching career had I found it necessary to remove a student from my class.

PIONEERS 9: UPHEAVAL

They found the room was unchanged from the previous session. Before the trading recommenced Carberry allowed each group a few minutes to take stock of their current situation and plan their strategy.

"You won't get any more uranium," said Patsy.

"And why not?"

"I was talking to Roger after the last session…"

"You've no right to talk to him about our business!" Darren snarled.

"I'll talk to whoever I want to." Patsy showed a rare flash of anger. "Anyway, he doesn't trust you."

"Sensible bloke," said Nikki.

"You shut up!"

"And you've had your last poison plant. I'm not getting you any more." Patsy stood her ground.

Darren could barely contain his fury, "If you won't then I'm taking over the trading. You bitches can stay here!" He turned to Simeon, "You look after them!"

Simeon was taken totally by surprise. "Yes, er, er…yeah."

"Enjoy yourself, slug!" said Nikki. "C'mon, we're off." She

gathered her bag and stood up, together with Tina and Patsy, and, tentatively, by Lizzie.

"Where are you going?" shrieked Simeon.

"We're defecting. You tossers can play your own pathetic games." said Nikki.

Darren barred their way. "No fucking way you're leaving! Sit down!"

"Piss off!" Nikki hissed.

Tom and Steve restrained Darren back as he tried to grab her. "Not worth it. Let them go." said Tom.

Darren shook them off. "Bitch! Nobody treats me like that."

Carberry was on the point of intervening when he saw the girls walk away from Darren's group. He beckoned them over. "What was that all about?" he asked.

"We've had enough of him," said Tina, "We want to join Roger's group."

"If that's okay with you, sir," Patsy added. "We'll be, um, like refugees or asylum seekers."

"And he wants to take over the world," said Lizzie, "I heard him say so."

"What do you mean?" Carberry was clearly disturbed by the turn of events.

"He's making an atom bomb and poison gas."

"You don't know that, Lizzie," said Tina.

"It's true, he is!" Lizzie was getting agitated.

"All right, calm down now," said Carberry. "Leave it with me." He took a deep breath. "Have you already spoken to Roger about this?"

"Sort of," said Patsy, "I told him we'd all had enough of Darren. He said we could always leave."

"Mmm." Carberry thought for a moment. "Okay, Patsy, you

go and talk to Roger. If he's happy to take you all in, I have no objection. I suggest though that you take a passive role with them for the time being."

Despite his simmering anger over the girls' defection, Darren was feeling quite pleased with himself. He had managed through a combination of charm, bribery and deceit, to persuade Delta and Theta to part with any poison plant they held. Although Epsilon, on Roger's direction, had refused to deal directly with him, he also managed to acquire more uranium that had previously been exchanged by them with another group. He felt ready to launch his coup.

Until Simeon handed him the latest card.

"Bastard!" he exploded, "I'm not having this!"

As Darren stormed over to Carberry's desk, Tom and Steve looked on in bewilderment, "What's set him off now, Sim?"

"Dunno, I didn't look at it."

Darren waved the card angrily in Carberry's face. "You're doing this on purpose! You were doing it on the space journey, deliberately obstructing us, and you're still doing it!"

Carberry took the card from Darren's hand and looked at it. He then sifted through the stack of remaining cards for each community, and extracted a few. "Sit down, Darren," he said calmly.

"I don't want to…"

"SIT DOWN!" Carberry rarely raised his voice.

Apart from a few hushed whispers, the class descended into silence, waiting to see what happened next. Darren opened his mouth to voice his defiance, thought better of it, and reluctantly took one of the vacant chairs in front of Carberry's desk.

"Thank you." Carberry then addressed the whole group. "I'd

like the leaders of each group to join me, and everyone else to return to base."

When the four leaders, including Darren, were seated in from of him, Carberry fanned out the selected cards for them to view. "You will remember last week I told you there would be a few surprises in store. As you can see, these cards describe a number of natural disasters and man-made crises. They do not necessarily affect every community. They were shuffled and distributed at random between your groups along with other resource and discussion cards. Darren was the first to encounter one of these cards and unfortunately the earthquake card does apply to the Omega community.

Carberry allowed the students a short time to examine the cards before continuing, "Darren thinks that I have treated his group unfairly, so to eliminate any possibility of bias I am going to shuffle these cards again and ask him to select one. The rest will be shared out between the groups. You will now all be aware in advance of some problems your community may face, if you are unlucky."

Carberry held out the shuffled cards, "Darren?"

With ill grace Darren picked a card, glanced at it, and flung it to the floor. "Shit!" He stood up abruptly, knocking the chair over, "Stuff your bloody cards!" he yelled, walking over the door and flinging it wide. He strode out slamming the door behind him.

"Shall we get on with our business?" Carberry said apparently unperturbed by the outburst. "Stephen," he called, "would you please go and find Darren. He had better be outside my door before the end of this lesson."

"Christ, I can see why Darren lost his cool," said Tom, studying the card, which Steve had handed him before leaving on his search.

"Why, what's it say?" asked Simeon.

"Radiation leak. We can't use any uranium and half of our plant resources are destroyed."

"He can't do that!" Simeon yelped.

"No choice. You saw what happened. Darren's luck ran out." Tom thought for a moment. "But we have a problem, Sim. There's just the two of us, until Steve returns. I'm going to ask the girls to come back."

"No way!" Simeon protested. "Darren put me in charge."

"Darren's not here. Anyway, have you got a better idea?"

"I, er…, we could, um…Not really,"

"Right then, go and ask Patsy. On second thoughts, I'll do it," said Tom, sensing Simeon's reluctance.

Some fifteen minutes later, in the midst of frenetic activity as Deltans coped with flooding and the Thetans were recovering from a devastating forest fire, Steve sloped back into the room. He signalled with his thumb to Carberry that Darren was on his way.

Shortly afterwards Darren stood in the doorway, glowering. Patsy, Tina and Nikki were in close discussion with Tom while Simeon snapped round the group like a terrier trying to exert his non-existent authority. Steve sprawled on a chair, taking little interest in the proceedings, and Lizzie hovered nervously on the fringe.

Carberry intercepted Darren's purposeful move to rejoin the group. "Outside, Darren. Now!"

"You can…"

Carberry gave him no chance to finish. "You will wait outside until we're finished here. You will take no further part in the proceedings until you have leant to control your temper… and your language."

"My group…" Darren started to protest.

"Are managing very well without you. Now go."

Behind Carberry's back, Nikki contemptuously gave Darren two fingers.

Darren made a threatening gesture in her direction then turned and strode out.

LIZZIE'S DIARY 9

Darren was really angry. Patsy wouldn't get him any more uranium for his atom bomb. I'm pleased though, I didn't want to get blown up. Mr Carberry didn't seem worried when I told him. Perhaps he didn't believe me. Nobody really takes any notice of what I say.

I was quite frightened because I thought Darren was going to hit Mr Carberry. He should have sent Darren out straight away but instead he made him sit down and play cards. That was really weird. They weren't proper cards, of course, only some like the ones we'd been using on our planet. I'm surprised that Mr Carberry let him go first in choosing a card – I'd have made him go last for being so horrible. But Darren started swearing and stormed out of the room. I'm glad he wasn't allowed to come back in.

Tom asked us to go back and help because Nikki had tried to get us to join Roger's group when Darren lost his temper.

Mr Carberry told us that our journey would soon be over. We'll have to pop back home anyway for the disco tonight.

I don't really want to go back into space.

SPACETALK

Tina Wilson@cando
@nikotinegirl @PatClem Chill out. CU both at disco 8 pm

Nikki Ridley@nikotinegirl
@cando May b late. Lift with Dad if home

Patsy Clements@PatClem
@cando C u there

Tina Wilson@cando
@nikotinegirl no worries. C u whenever

MISSION CONTROL 10

I'd threatened to bar Darren from any further participation in the simulation. With only another couple of sessions remaining until the debriefing and analysis, I was, however, reluctant to exclude him permanently from the process. I had given him the option of undertaking to reform his behaviour.

Bereft of an audience of his peers, I'd always found Darren quite responsive and sensible on a one-to-one basis. And so it proved when I confronted him on his own after the class had been dismissed. He accepted that his behaviour had been out of order and readily apologised to me for his aggressive attitude.

I agreed that he could rejoin the group in the next session after half term when I assumed passions would have cooled down. I was intending to wind down myself with a week in Wales, undertaking preparatory work for the Easter field trip.

PIONEERS 10:
END GAME

"Beats me why they call it a Hallowe'en Ball," said Tina to Patsy. "It's not on the thirty-first of October."

"Near enough though," said Patsy. "Makes sense to hold it on the Friday before half term. And the sixth-formers do make an effort to decorate the hall."

"Yeah, paper bats and spiders from the lower school art classes. And they're not even allowed to come until they're in year 9. They have their own weeny hop in the afternoon, remember?"

"Yeah, pretty gross," said Patsy, wrinkling her nose. "Is Nikki coming?"

"Yeah. May be a bit late though, depends when her Dad gets home from work."

The hall was beginning to fill up with small groups, mostly single sex from years 9 and 10. Few had bothered to wear any of the permitted ghoulish masks. Several older students – those who had come with a partner – were the only ones yet dancing under the strobe lights.

"There's Nikki!" Tina waved. "Oh, would you believe it, she's got Lizzie following her like a poodle. Pathetic!"

Quite what image Nikki intended to project was uncertain. The black top, black short skirt, black tights, black lipstick and eyeliner to complement her long black hair were certainly in keeping with the theme of the evening.

Darren had been lounging just inside the door with Steve and Simeon. Spotting Nikki, he stood up quickly and made to bar her entry. "Well, if it isn't the black witch," he sneered.

"Bet she'd like to ride your broomstick," Steve sniggered.

"Piss off, morons," Nikki said.

Darren poked her in the chest. "You pissed me off, you bitch," he growled, "You made me look a fool this afternoon."

"You didn't need my help," Nikki retorted, "Carbunkle give you a bollocking, did he?"

"Leave her alone, Darren," Patsy said.

"Leave her alone," Darren mimicked, "Miss Bloody Perfect! Blabbing away our plans to Carbunkle and that Simpson prick. Sweet talking Tom into letting you take over."

"As it happens, I didn't say anything about your stupid plans." Patsy said heatedly.

"And Tom's got more common sense than you'll ever have," said Nikki

Darren grabbed her arm and twisted it behind her back.

"Take your fucking hands off me!" she squealed.

"Do as she says, Darren." said Roger, who had just arrived and quickly taken in the situation.

"Mind you own fucking business!"

Alerted by Lizzie, the School Counsellor and disco organiser, Tony Stanford, intervened. "Rooney, let go of her! Now! And unless you want to be chucked out now I suggest that you calm down and behave yourself. You won't get another warning."

Darren released his grip and slouched away, muttering

obscenities under his breath and brushing away Steve's attempts to mollify him.

"Don't let him spoil the evening," said Roger. "Take a spell on the floor, Patsy?"

Patsy let him lead her into the midst of the young people now gyrating and swaying to the music. As Tina and Nikki also began to dance, Simeon forced himself between them, waggling his fat backside to the beat of the music.

"Get lost, Sim," Nikki shouted to make herself heard. The volume had been slowly cranked up to a level at which normal conversation was impossible.

"I've as much right…"

"Just shift your arse somewhere else," said Nikki.

"Wondered when you were going to turn up, " said Darren, pushing himself away from the wall near the soft drinks bar where he and Steve had lounged for over half an hour. They'd made no attempt to join in the dancing.

"Sorry, had a puncture on my bike," said Tom.

Darren tossed an empty coke can in the bin. "I've had enough of this piss. Need something stronger."

Tom looked concerned, "We're not allowed to go into town or bring any alcohol in."

"No problem. I've got a stash of booze out the back. They can't stop us going outside for fresh air if they think we can't escape."

"Where have you hidden it?" asked Steve.

"You know that old bunker behind the bike sheds? Where they keep grit for the paths? I smuggled in some cans of lager this morning. C'mon I'll show you."

Tom looked round, "What about Sim? Isn't he here?"

"Bugger Sim."

"Probably trying to impress some bitch with his dancing," said Steve. "Saw he got the brush off from Nikki and Tina a while back."

"You're not serious?" said Tom.

"Fat chance!" said Darren, "Don't think anyone would be that desperate. Even Lizzie."

"Time for a fag," Nikki announced when she'd extricated herself from the swaying mass of bodies still dancing. "Do you want one, Tinny?"

"No thanks, I'll pass. Take care then. Darren's still around."

"I'll be back soon. I don't think he'd be that stupid."

Simeon watched Nikki make her way to the double doors, which led out to a quadrangle and thence to the numerous temporary classrooms, various outbuildings and the playing fields. Although the main entrance to the school was supervised all evening and anyone leaving was not allowed to return to the disco, there were no checks on access to the rest of the school campus, since, in theory, it was securely enclosed.

Simeon looked round, and, seeing no sign of Darren, on impulse sloped out after Nikki. He saw her heading towards the bike sheds but then, perhaps because she'd detected someone else already there, she suddenly turned onto the path between two long prefabricated buildings.

Though the weather had been mild for most of the month, the clear skies augured well for a frosty night. Lizzie shivered in the chill autumn air, unsure what to do. She'd had been outside for some time looking in vain for Nikki to tell her she would make her own way home. She didn't want to wait another hour or more for a lift back with Nikki's dad. When Darren and his two cronies appeared, she'd hidden, not daring to get closer to the bike sheds where they were talking. Her spirits rose as she caught sight of Nikki leaving the main building. On the point of calling out to her friend, she held back, thinking that Nikki would not welcome attention if she was coming out to smoke. Nor did she want to alert Darren or even Simeon, who had left the hall soon after Nikki.

"Just going for a leak," said Darren. "Don't nick the rest of the beer." He belched, and tossed an empty can into the bunker.

Nikki only became aware that she was not alone the moment before her arm was grabbed from behind. "What the…" Nikki cried. As her assailant attempted to spin her round, she lost her balance and fell, striking the back of her head on the concrete path.

Seeing her lying on the path, moaning softly, Simeon felt a strange sensation in his groin. Her short skirt had ridden up during her fall, exposing the top of her thighs. No girl had ever let him get anywhere near enough to be intimate. On an impulse, he knelt down and tugged at her black tights, ripping them and as he slid his hand under the top of her underwear, fumbling, he tensed and felt an involuntary release of sticky fluid into his pants.

"Stop it!, stop it!" Lizzie yelled, " You're hurting her!"

Simeon scrambled to his feet and scuttled off across the playing field.

"Hear that?" said Tom.

"Yeah," said Steve, "Some bitch yelping."

"Think we should see what's up?"

"What about Darren?"

Tom was already striding off.

"Where're we going?" Steve belched loudly as he made to follow.

Darren emerged from the darkness, and caught up with Tom. "Know what's happened?"

"No, but we heard a girl scream, sounded like she was behind the cowsheds." Tom used the common knickname for the temporary classrooms. They broke into a trot.

"Bloody hell, it's Nikki!" yelled Tom, "She's been hurt!" He bent down beside her and felt for a pulse.

"Is...is she dead?" Steve stammered.

"No, thank Christ, she's still breathing." Tom took off his hoodie and covered her exposed lower body. "We need to call an ambulance."

"My phone's dead," Darren grunted.

Tom fumbled in his pocket for his mobile phone and held it out to Darren. "Here, use mine!"

"Shouldn't we wait for one of the teachers?" said Steve.

"You go and find somebody," Tom said impatiently. "Darren, give me your coat. We need to keep her warm."

Reluctantly Darren handed Tom his leather jacket. "Stupid tart," he muttered.

They both turned when they heard Steve call out, "Over there!" and several people appeared from the behind the main school end of the temporary classroom.

Roger took just one glance at Nikki's body lying motionless. "You sick bastard!" he yelled at Darren and swung his fist, striking him full in the face.

Darren staggered back, clutching his nose, now streaming with blood. Roger went for him again, almost landing another blow to his jaw.

"He didn't do anything to her!" Steve shouted, holding Roger back with Tom's help. "It wasn't him!"

"Right, back off, the lot of you!" Tony Stanford panted breathlessly. "Stand back!"

Tina and Patsy watched at a respectable distance while he examined Nikki's injuries. He grimaced and called to his colleague, music teacher Mary Watkins. "I think it would be best if no students are allowed to leave the premises just yet. Get everyone back inside and organise a roll call."

They all heard the sirens of the approaching ambulance. One was permanently based at the cottage hospital in Merton Stoke, but except for the most minor of injuries, casualties were usually taken to the nearest A & E unit some fifteen miles away.

Simeon looked back when he reached the oak trees on the far side of the playing field. He realised with horror he was being followed, though in the weak moonlight he couldn't recognise his pursuer. With no good places to hide he knew the only way to avoid discovery was to get over the wooden fence into the lane beyond. Frantically, he scrambled through clumps of nettles and bramble along the border searching for a way of escaping. In desperation he kicked at a section of rotten timber to enlarge a hole big enough to crawl through.

"Stop!"

Simeon raised his hands to protect his eyes from the beam of Lizzie's pocket LED torch. But he recognised her voice and relaxed, perceiving no threat.

"Well, our little mouse. Bit late for Mummy to let you out, isn't it?" he sneered.

"Your hurt my friend!"

"Nah, the slut was asking for it."

"Don't say that! You hurt her!" Lizzie shrieked.

"Jealous you didn't get some?" Simeon said, growing in confidence. "Not that anyone would want to do it with you."

"I hate you! I hate you!" Lizzie lunged at Simeon, her nail scissors pricking his arm through his jacket."

"Ouch! You stupid bitch!" Simeon backed away, and stumbled.

In a frenzy, Lizzie stabbed again and again at Simeon as he cowered on the ground trying to protect himself. Blood began to seep through his clothing and from a cut to his cheek.

"Aw, shit, stop, stop it, you crazy f..." he squealed, his face contorted in pain. "Aaah!" Another blow dug through the flesh of Simeon's nose. He fainted.

The sudden strong odour of Simeon's bowel movement caused Lizzie to pause. As she stared at his blood stained motionless body and at her own hands covered in his gore, the enormity of her actions began to dawn. In panic, she threw down her scissors and scrambled through the gap Simeon had made in the fence, her small body passing through where he would have struggled.

The paramedic took Tony Stanford to one side. "The police should be called in on this. She's been sexually assaulted."

"You mean raped?" Tony held his head, dreading the consequences.

"I don't think so, but certainly looks as if someone was trying."

"Is she going to be all right?"

"Probably concussed. She's had a nasty bang on the head but her pulse is strong and her breathing's steady. She'll be given a scan at the hospital just to check there's no internal damage."

"What about the lad? Doesn't he need to go hospital too?"

"He'll be okay. More damage to his pride I'd say. Get his parents to take him to the hospital tomorrow if they're concerned. We can't take him in the ambulance."

One less worry, Tony thought. One student in hospital was serious enough. He escorted Darren back to the main building and to the first aid room."Keep an eye on him," he instructed a sixth former, "He's not to leave the room."

After a call to the police, Tony joined his colleague in the hall. Some students were still lined up waiting for Mary Watkins to check off their names on form lists, while the others swayed unenthusiastically to the disco music now operating at much reduced volume under normal lighting. Darren and Nikki's friends pressed up to Tony Stanford, anxious for news.

"Just give me a minute, please." he said. He signalled to the disc jockey, who faded out the music and offered Tony a microphone. The hall fell silent.

"I'm sorry to tell you that one of our students has been involved in an accident. She has been taken to hospital but her condition is not thought to be serious. Unfortunately there is some uncertainty about what actually happened, and we have been advised to inform the police."

There was an audible gasp from the assembly.

"I'm afraid that it means you will not be allowed to leave until they get here. Now most of you have already given your name to Mrs Watkins, and we have your addresses, so there shouldn't be a problem. If you were expecting to be picked up before the end of the disco then you might like to text or phone to say you'll be staying later. I would appreciate it however if you do not mention the reason. Just say you're having a good time."

But he could see from their faces that the fun factor was not likely to return that evening.

"A couple more points. If you have been outside for any reason at any time this evening please go over to the foyer now. And if there is anyone you know that was here earlier – perhaps came with you to the disco – but is not in this hall now, I want to know."

"I suppose we'll be in the shit for drinking?" Steve said to Tom. From a group of a dozen or so that had left the disco and gone outside, they, along with Roger, Tina and Patsy, were the only students that had been asked to remain in the foyer.

"Perhaps, but the focus is going to be on Nikki."

"And Darren," Tina butted in.

"Why? He didn't do anything." said Steve.

"Not what you saw, was it, Roger?"

"Dead right!" Roger felt his bruised knuckles.

"He was trying to help her!" Steve insisted. "I was there too!"

"Yeah, sure. Think anyone will believe him?" said Tina. She thought for a moment. "Have any of you seen Lizzie recently?"

They all shook their heads. "Didn't know she'd come," said Tom.

"She came with Nikki, I think," said Patsy.

"And what about your fat friend?" Tina asked. "Haven't seen him since we told him to piss off."

"Perhaps he and Lizzie have run away together," Steve chuckled, "Those two losers are just made for each other."

"That's not even remotely funny!" said Tina hotly.

"Still, we'd better let Mr Stanford know," Patsy nodded in the direction of the first aid room from where the teacher had just emerged, followed by a policeman.

"Thank you for waiting."

"As if we had a choice," Steve muttered.

"Now PC Tunbridge has the general picture of what happened this evening, but the police will obviously want to investigate further how Nikki was injured."

"Is Nikki okay?" asked Tina anxiously.

"Yes, I've heard that she's recovered consciousness, and her parents are with her in the hospital."

"Can we visit her?" said Patsy.

"If I may?" the constable interceded, "Yes, of course you will be able to visit your friend, but we would like to talk to her and to each of you first."

"And what about Darren?" asked Tom, "What's happening to him?"

"I've been trying to contact his parents. We'd really like them to come in."

"He's got no mum and his dad's always pissed. He'll be in the pub till he gets chucked out," said Tom. "Darren more or less looks after himself."

"I see." Tony thought for a moment, and spoke to the officer, "Is it okay if I arrange to take him to the hospital for a check up first? I'll try again to get in touch with his father but if he isn't in any fit state to accompany his son, I'll bring him to the police station tomorrow morning."

"Yes, he should have some responsible adult present when he is being questioned."

"Will we all have to go to the police station tonight?" Tina asked

"Probably not. I think we can leave it till tomorrow. I have your addresses."

"Sir," said Patsy, " You asked us to tell you if any of our friends are missing."

"Yes?"

"We haven't seen Lizzie Humphrey since she arrived with Nikki, and Simeon's not here either."

"Could either of them have gone home early?" asked PC Tunbridge.

"One moment, I'll check with the stewards on the gate," said Tony.

"Where do your two friends live?" PC Tunbridge asked, "Could they have walked home?"

"Sim lives in town," said Tom.

"Lizzie's a couple of miles out, not that far, but she gets the bus in to school," said Patsy.

"And what are they like? Popular?"

"Hardly. They're both wimps," said Steve. "Sim usually hangs around with us two and Darren."

"Is it possible they could have gone off together somewhere?"

"No way!"

"Hmm. Well, we need to establish their whereabouts. We'll need to talk to them as well."

Tony Stanford returned looking worried. "The gate stewards haven't seen them. I've rung their parents, and neither youngster has returned home yet. Any ideas?" he said to the students.

"When we found..." Tom looked at Stanford unsure whether to continue.

"Go on."

"When we found Nikki, I thought...I mean, it's possible... someone was running across the school field."

"Typical, trying to shift the blame," muttered Roger.

"Right, I'll take a look anyway," said the constable.

"Can we go home now?" asked Tina.

"Yes, I don't think there's any need for you to hang around any longer. We have your contact details."

The disco had been allowed to continue but few students had shown any inclination to dance any more after they had been given permission to leave. Those who were relying on parents or friends for transport to outlying villages were still milling around awaiting the fast approaching official finish time.

For the second time that evening, the road to the school was lit up by flashing blue lights.

Lizzie had walked along the tree-lined country road many times in daylight but never in the dark. And never on her own. But she was more terrified of being seen bloodstained and dishevelled than by the black shadows and sounds of the woodland wildlife at night. She hid whenever she saw distant headlights.

Without a wristwatch or mobile of her own she had no idea of the passing time. She sighed with relief when eventually the isolated stone cottage where she lived with her mother came into view. There was a light in her mother's bedroom.

She carefully put her key in the door and padded softly up the stairs.

"That you dear?" her mother called.

"Yes, Mum."

"Glad you're home. I was getting worried. The school rang earlier."

Lizzie felt her heart leap. She closed her bedroom door and flung herself on the bed, sobbing quietly. Until she heard the door bell ring. She froze. She heard her mother bustling along the landing and calling, "I'm coming, coming!"

"Who is it?" said Mrs Humphrey.

"Police, madam. May we have a word?"

Mrs Humphrey opened the door as far as the security chain would permit.

"Well?"

"Has your daughter arrived back home yet?"

"Yes."

"How long ago?"

"Not long, I suppose. She went with her friend Nikki."

"Did you see her come in?"

"No but I spoke to her."

"And she answered?"

"Yes."

"Could you have a word with her?"

"She went straight to sleep, poor thing. Surely you don't expect me to wake her up?"

"We will need to speak with her tomorrow morning."

"Why? What's this all about? Lizzie's a good girl."

The police officer hesitated for a moment, weighing up what to say. "It is possible she may have witnessed an assault on another student. She may...ah...have been frightened and run away."

LIZZIE'S DIARY 10

I wish I hadn't gone to the disco. Mum didn't want me to. But all the others were going, and I didn't want to let Patsy down.

It was horrible. All flashing lights and noise, like something from Dr Who, or Mr Carberry's spacemen, but he wasn't there. You couldn't speak to anybody even if you wanted to. And nobody wanted to speak to me anyway. I'm not much good at dancing. I'm not really much good at anything.

I wanted to go home. I didn't mind walking. I couldn't bear waiting until Nikki's Dad came to pick us up. I was going to tell her but I couldn't see her in the hall. I think she smokes behind the bike sheds.

He was hurting Nikki. I saw Sim kneel on top of her. He must have stuffed something over her mouth to stop her screaming. He had his hand up her skirt.

I yelled at him to stop, and he ran off. I didn't think. I just followed him. I was scared but I got my nail scissors out my bag just in case.

He just laughed when I caught up with him. He called me dirty names and said nasty things about my friend. I've never been so angry before.

I think I've killed him. I suppose I should be sorry but I'm not.

I wish Mr Carberry hadn't made us go to that horrible planet. None of this would have happened.

I'm not going to let them send me to prison. I'm not going to write anything else. Ever.

ENQUIRY 1

When Simeon had staggered, dirty and bleeding, into the arms of PC Tunbridge the previous evening, the police had realised that they were facing a far more complex investigation. And taking statements from a number of students was now far more urgent.

The Headmaster had not been at all pleased to be intercepted when he had arrived home from a Rotary dinner, particularly as he'd been a little less than prudent with the wine. Reluctantly, however, he agreed to make the school available on the Saturday morning for the police to conduct interviews. They suggested that students, accompanied by their parents, were less likely to feel intimidated in familiar surroundings than hanging around at the police station, which in any case would have meant an hour's round journey. Beside which, they would be able to build up a much better picture of who had been where and why. Tony Stanford agreed to act as the responsible adult in loco parentis if necessary.

Nikki hadn't been able to give the police any information about her attacker. She had been kept in hospital overnight for observation.

Cleaned up, stitched and bandaged, Simeon had eventually been allowed to go home, but had steadfastly refused to give any explanation at the time of how he had got into such a state.

Another police officer was visiting Simeon again at home at the same time as the interviews at the school.

D.I. Robbins invited Darren and the school counsellor to take a seat. "Darren, you have the right to have your father present during this interview, but I understand he has agreed to Mr Stanford taking his place?"

"Yeah, Dad would be useless."

"You know that we are trying to find out what happened to Nikki Ridley and to Simeon Parks…"

"What's happened to Sim?" Darren said, puzzled.

"Some cuts and bruises, Darren," said Stanford. "He'll be okay."

"As I was saying," continued the detective, "we don't know who assaulted Nikki, but you were seen standing by her body. Therefore I have to give you a formal caution." He recited the familiar miranda phrases. "Do you understand?"

"Yeah but I didn't do anything to her, for Christ's sake! She was already on the ground. I was trying to help."

"But you lost your temper with her earlier in the evening, didn't you?"

"She's a lippy bitch." Darren glanced at Tony Stanford. "She's been getting up my nose all the time in Carbu…Mr Carberry's stupid spaceship game," he added. "But it wasn't me that hurt her last night."

DC Robbins turned to Stanford and raised an eyebrow, "Know about this game?"

"Vaguely. Simulation exercise I think. You'll have to ask Martyn Carberry yourself."

"Right, I will. Darren, can you please tell me why you were outside that evening."

"We'd gone – that's Steve and Tom as well – to, er, get some fresh air."

"Are you sure that's all?"

Darren looked anxiously at Stanford, "Well, I'd hidden some cans of beer behind the bike sheds. S'ppose I'll get into trouble for that."

"I think you've got more serious problems to sort out first, Darren," said Tony Stanford.

"So tell me what happened next."

"We heard a girl shout."

"Do you know who it was? And what did she say?"

"Don't know. Tom heard her."

"What did you do?"

"We went to where we thought the sound had come from. We saw someone on the ground."

"And this was where?"

"At the field end of some temporary classrooms. Nikki was lying there. I think she'd hit her head."

"Did you interfere with her?"

"What do you mean?" Darren bristled.

"Did you touch her under her skirt?"

"I'm not a bloody pervert!" Darren shouted. "No I didn't. Her skirt was up round her waist though. Not that she had much of a skirt anyway," he said more calmly.

"What did you do then?"

"Tom checked to see if she was still breathing. And I phoned for an ambulance." Darren breathed deeply. "Look, I know you think I attacked her in some way but in that case I'm hardly likely to have hung around. I wanted to help."

"You were punched on the nose. Why do you think that happened?"

"I guess Roger thought the same as you, that I'd attacked Nikki."

The inspector's mobile trilled. "Excuse me a moment." He

stood up and moved over to the door. He frowned as he listened to the caller. "Well, you'd better get over there right away." He terminated the call. "Darren, I think we're done for the time being but I'd appreciate it if you stay around the school for a while in case we have any further questions after we've tried to corroborate your story."

D.I. Robbins waited until Darren had left. "Mr Stanford, I've just heard that Simeon Parks is claiming that a girl called Lizzie Humphrey stabbed him with scissors."

"Lizzie? That's ridiculous. She wouldn't hurt a fly."

"Any idea why he'd say that?"

"Not at all. Unless he'd tried to assault her. But that's not likely either."

"I've sent an officer round to her house to see what she has to say." He rubbed his eyes. "Meanwhile, let's press on."

Steve Tancock and Tom Anson had little to add, merely confirming what Darren had already said.

"Tom, you heard a girl scream, correct?"

"Not really a scream, more like a shout."

"And you've no idea who it was?"

"That's right."

"Did you see anyone else, apart from Nikki, that is?"

"I think someone was on the sports field but I can't be sure. It was too dark to see properly."

"You didn't try to follow?"

"No, I gave Darren my mobile and sent Steve to fetch help."

Roger was the next to be interviewed.

"Did you punch Darren Rooney?"

Roger looked at his father, unsure whether to commit himself.

"You don't need to worry. Darren won't be making a formal complaint."

"Yes, I hit him."

"Why?"

"I thought he'd been having a go at Nikki again."

"Again? What do you mean by that?"

"When I got to the disco he'd really lost it. He'd grabbed her arm and was swearing at her."

"Do you know why?"

"The two of them have been at each other's throats for the last few weeks. It spilled over from Mr Carberry's lesson today. He's a Geography teacher."

"Just in his lesson?"

"Pretty much so."

The inspector looked puzzled. "And what is it about his lessons that generate such strong feelings? I always found Geography pretty boring."

"Well, it's an extended role play thing. We're supposed to be astronauts and we've landed on another planet similar to Earth."

"Right. Well I don't propose to ask you to go into what you think Mr Carberry had in mind in doing this, but why should Darren and Nikki get so worked up?"

"They ended up, accidentally really, in the same group. Darren likes to be in charge and Nikki doesn't take to being bossed around."

"And who else is in the same group?"

"Darren's mates, Tom Anson and Steve Tancock. Simeon Parks hangs on their coat tails. Then there's Nikki, Tina Wilson, Patsy Clements and Lizzie Humphrey."

"But not you?"

"No, There's eight of us in another group." Roger paused, then added, "In the last session, the girls wanted to join our group."

"Leave Darren's lot, you mean?"

"Yes."

"And did they?"

"For a short time. Until Darren stormed out after arguing with Mr Carberry. He wouldn't let Darren back in."

"Then what?"

"Tom asked the girls to come back."

"Hmm. Interesting. Okay, thank you for your help."

D.I. Robbins decided to take a break before interviewing Nikki's friends. His mobile rang again.

"Wake up, Lizzie, dear. There's a police lady would like to speak to you," Mrs Humphrey tapped on her daughter's bedroom door. "She's usually up by now," she twittered to the two officers waiting at the bottom of the stairs, "but she was late home last night so I let her sleep in."

Mrs Humphrey knocked harder, "Lizzie, come on, love." With no response she reached for the door handle. "Lizzie, I'm coming in!"

The door wouldn't open. "Lizzie, open this door at once!" Her hand flew to her mouth as she remembered there were no locks on the bedroom doors. "The door's jammed!"

The police officers rushed up the stairs in concern. The WPC took Mrs Humphrey to one side while her male colleague tried the door. "I'll have to force it," he said.

He put his shoulder against the door and pushed, then gave a hard shove. A desk on the other side squeaked and yielded enough for the policeman to squeeze through. "Wait!" he commanded.

He rushed over to the young girl lying sprawled face down on the bed, noting the two empty pill bottles on the floor. He took her limp wrist to check for a pulse while calling in on his radio. "Emergency! Young girl, suspected overdose. Need to get her to hospital urgently. She's still alive, just."

"Lizzie! Lizzie!" her mother shrieked, "Lizzie, my love, what have you done!"

D.I. Robbins looked grim. He wasn't sure how the two girls would react. He decided to talk to the two girls and their parents together.

"I'm afraid I have some very sad news," he began.

"Not Nikki!" cried Tina, " Tell me, Nikki's all right. Please!"

"Nikki's fine. It's Lizzie."

Patsy and Tina looked at each other, puzzled. "What do you mean?" Patsy asked.

"It looks like she took an overdose. She never regained consciousness. She died in the ambulance on the way to hospital. I'm sorry."

Patsy held her hands to her face, sobbing uncontrollably, while her mother tried to comfort her.

Tina just sat staring, mouth open in shock. "But...but... why?"

"We don't know yet. But it is possible that she may have been responsible for injuries to Simeon."

"Lizzie? That just doesn't make sense! She wouldn't hurt anybody."

"Look, I know this is very difficult for you, but it would help if you could tell me a little about her. You were her friends, right?"

"Not really," said Tina, "She didn't really have any friends. She was a bit of a wimp. Sorry, Patsy, but it is true."

"Not even Nikki?"

"They travelled on the same bus together. Nikki sort of tolerated her."

"But she was in your group on this spaceship thing in Geography?"

147

"No, that was in Current Affairs! Yes, Patsy took pity on her."

Patsy raised her head, her eyes red with tears. "I felt sorry for her. All she needed was a bit of TLC. She was harmless. Took things a bit too literally, though."

"Do you mean she was simple minded? Sorry, I don't mean to malign her but I do need to get some idea of her state of mind."

"Not simple," said Patsy, "more naïve."

"And not streetwise, if you know what I mean," said Tina.

The inspector decided against pursuing Tina's description for the time being. "So what reason do you think she might have had for attacking Simeon?"

"No idea."

"Could she have attacked Nikki as well?"

"That's an absolutely stupid suggestion!" declared Tina hotly. "Sorry, I mean ridiculous."

"Jealousy perhaps?"

"I don't think Lizzie would know how to be jealous. And she certainly wouldn't be jealous of Sim."

"They didn't like each other?"

"Sim's a moron. No-one likes him. Mostly we just ignore him."

"Okay," D.I. Robbins leaned back in his chair and ran his hands through his thinning hair. "You've been very helpful. I certainly don't have a clear understanding yet of what exactly happened last night but I'm getting some of the picture. I will need to find out what else Simeon and Nikki can tell me."

"When can we see her?" asked Tina.

"I believe she's been allowed home now, so perhaps you'd like to give her parents a ring?"

The Headmaster, Dr Charles Hallam, approached the inspector impatiently as soon as he emerged from the interview room.

"Have you finished here now?" he said abruptly, then added more co-operatively, "I mean, is there any way I can be of further assistance?"

"We're more or less done for the time being, thank you. My officers have completed a search of the grounds and if we do need to talk to any of the students again we can do so at their home or possibly the station."

"Are any of my students likely to face charges?" Dr Hallam sounded surprised.

"We can't say yet, but with a young girl and a lad both hospitalised after a serious assault, it's certainly possible. And we also need to consider whether they have any bearing on why another student apparently took her own life."

"What! Why have I not been informed?"

"I myself have only just been told. I do not have any further details at the moment."

"This is terrible...terrible for the school. Reporters are already pestering me for comments about the...the assaults."

D.I. Robbins held back from voicing his thought that the headmaster seemed far more concerned about his image and the school that about grieving parents. "I'd be grateful if you could provide me with a contact for one of your teaching staff, Mr Carberry."

"Oh, why's that?" Dr Hallam said brusquely.

"It is possible that something which happened during his lessons may be linked in some way to last night's tragic events. We need to speak to him."

"Hah, I always thought his project would lead to trouble! He'll have me to answer to for bringing the school into disrepute."

"I wouldn't jump to conclusions yet, Dr Hallam, there may be nothing to it at all."

"We'll see!"

Simeon was obviously uncomfortable at having a second visit from the police that day. His mother, too, protested loudly, "Why do you have to keep pestering him? Can't you see he's still in pain? Have you arrested the girl that attacked him?"

"Mrs Parks, please. It is necessary for us to cross-check various statements, particularly in the light of new information," D.I. Robbins tried to calm the woman.

"I don't want to talk to him!" Simeon whined.

"It would be better if you do answer my questions, but I have to advise you of your right not to do so." The inspector went through the formal caution.

"Why are you treating my son like a criminal?" Mrs Parks yelled, "He's the victim!"

"Yeah, what are you doing about that crazy bitch?" Simeon demanded.

"I'm sorry to tell you she's dead. Seems she took her own life."

"Serves her right!"

"Simeon! That's disrespectful, no matter what she did to you," his mother said sharply.

"We also have her diary." D.I. Robbins paused. "She claims to have seen you attacking Nikki Ridley."

"That's a lie! The bitch is lying!"

"She also wrote that she followed you and you taunted her, called her names."

"I didn't! She stabbed me with the scissors for no reason!"

"Lizzie Humphrey admits that she attacked you. Is that also a lie?"

"No, she did, she did!"

"And that was because you'd hurt her friend and she was very angry?"

"I didn't hurt anyone! She's crazy!"

"If you didn't sexually assault Nikki Ridley, why did the doctors find semen in your underclothes? Unless you were you trying it on with Lizzie, perhaps?"

"Not with her, no way!"

"With Nikki then?"

"Simeon, what did you do? Now tell the policeman the truth!"

"I...I..." Simeon looked ready to burst into tears, then rallied. "I found Nikki on the ground. I've...I've never seen a girl like that before...with her skirt up. I couldn't help it...it just happened."

"So you're telling me that you didn't push Nikki to the ground?"

"Yes, no, I didn't push her."

"Did you see who did, by any chance?" D.I. Robbins asked sceptically.

"Mr Carberry." .

Simeon could see that his answer had taken the inspector completely by surprise. Several seconds of silence passed before he put another question.

"Are you absolutely sure about that?"

"Yes. He fancied her."

"I think the little toerag's lying through his teeth," D.I. Robbins said later to his small team of officers working on the case, "but it's even more vital that we speak to this Carberry fellow."

"He's not at his home address," said PC Tunbridge. " We've

checked. Not answering the phone either. Lives on his own, apparently, no wife and kids."

"Any of his colleagues at school know where he might be?"

"Difficult with half term to contact them all. The Head and Tony Stanford, the Counsellor, didn't know."

"I wouldn't tell our Dr. Hallam anything I didn't have to," said D.I. Robbins. "But don't quote me on that!"

"Think he's done a runner, boss?" another plain-clothed officer asked.

"Possible. No-one's seen him since the end of school on Friday."

"Do we put out an alert? I mean, he could be dangerous."

The inspector considered the suggestion. "Not through the media. Let's keep it low-key at the moment. Circulate his photo, and if he's spotted anywhere, invite him to contact us as soon as possible. No need to say why, he'll know if he was directly involved in any way."

MISSION
ABORTED

The distinctly subdued, almost frosty atmosphere in the staff-room on Monday morning gave me the first inkling that my life was about to fall apart. Colleagues seemed to be avoiding me.

Except for Bob Hawkins, who took me aside and asked whether I knew what had really happened.

Having been away, I had no idea what he was talking about. I had felt no need to check my mobile phone, and I never bother with television or newspapers on my walking holidays.

I never made it to my classroom for registration. I was summoned to the Headmaster's office. Pending further investigations into the role of my irresponsible and dangerous project, as he put it, in causing serious assaults on three students and the tragic death of a young girl, I was to be suspended from my post, with immediate effect. Dr Hallam also seemed to take pleasure in declaring that the police were waiting to interview me.

I drove immediately to the police station, hoping that I could get some clear answers about events. I had no reason to suspect that they were looking to me for answers.

ENQUIRY 2

Assaults and a death involving children warranted front page headlines in the local papers. By the end of the half-term week even the nationals were beginning to pick up on a story that suggested, at the very least, unprofessional behaviour by a teacher and possibly a lot more.

Mrs Parks showed no hint of reticence in speaking to the press. She eagerly portrayed her son as the innocent victim, carefully avoiding any mention of his sexual indiscretions while allowing suspicion to fall upon Mr Carberry.

Dr. Hallam made all the right noises in public to offer condolences to the parents, and reassurances that measures would be put into place to ensure that such shocking events would never happen again at his school. He promised that a full internal investigation would take place and any member of staff who had behaved irresponsibly would face the consequences. When asked whether it was true that the police wished to interview Mr Carberry, his simple affirmative answer spoke volumes in the minds of the reporters at the press conference. In an attempt to minimise the media presence at the school premises he decreed that the three injured students should not return to school for another week, "To ensure they make a full recovery," he said.

Though Darren intended no personal malice, the mere mention of Martyn Carberry in his dismissive comments about the role-play sessions merely fuelled speculation in the media. They declared that something must have been seriously amiss in the young geography teacher's lessons and implied incitement to rape, grievous body harm and suicide. They also made much of the fact that the police had appaently been unable to trace him.

"Thank you, Mr Carberry, for coming in." D.I. Robbins gestured to him to take a seat. "You know why we want to talk to you?"

"I've only just heard about the terrible events at the disco. But other than give you my observations on the students involved, I'm not sure how I can help."

"Were you at the disco?"

"No, I've been in Wales. Walking. I only got back late last night."

"Really? And when did you leave?"

"Straight after school on Friday."

"Can anyone verify that? Were you travelling with someone?"

"No, I was on my own."

"And where did you stay?"

"I was camping."

"Bit cold for this time of year, isn't it?"

"I'm used to it."

"So can anyone confirm your whereabouts on the Friday evening?"

"Why should anyone need to?"

"One of the students claims he saw you outside the disco."

"That's impossible!"

"It's also claimed you assaulted Nikki Ridley."

"What!" Carberry shot up from the chair.

"Please sit down. Do you have a crush on her?"

"No I bloody well don't! Not on any of my students." Carberry took a deep breath to calm himself. He rarely lost his temper. "Look, I came in here, so I thought, to give perhaps some background to the students, not to be accused of being a pervert. I'm saying nothing more until I have a solicitor present."

"We are not accusing you of anything at the moment. Can you give us any proof that you were not at the school on the evening of the disco?"

Carberry thought for a moment. "It's possible the landlord of the pub might remember me. I went in for a quick drink after I'd pitched my tent. Weren't many people there. And, I did stop to fill up at a motorway services. I should have the receipt somewhere, and it will be on my credit card statement."

"Where was that, and what time?"

"Just over the Severn Bridge, about six o'clock, I suppose."

"And the pub?"

"In Crickhowell, the Bridge."

The inspector seemed satisfied with the answers. "That's easy to check, thank you. Just one more thing, can you tell us about the, um, project Nikki and others were doing in your lessons?"

"Yes I can, but I don't quite see what the relevance is to your enquiries."

"Lizzie, the girl who took her own life, kept a diary. She seems to blame your lessons for what happened. And the same project has been mentioned by other students."

Carberry blinked in astonishment. "Lizzie was never a problem. Okay, she wasn't the brightest spark but she kept a low profile, never got up to mischief."

"Was she bullied?"

"Not in my lessons. Patsy Clements tended to look after her."

"Any idea why she committed suicide?"

"Not a clue – not something I would ever have expected."

"Was there any cause for conflict in your lessons?"

"I expected that the very nature of the role play exercise would arouse some heated debate. It was something I intended to discuss in the debriefing sessions." Carberry added wistfully, "Doesn't look as if I'm going to get the chance to do that now."

"Did any particular students cause a problem?"

"I had to be pretty firm with Darren Rooney on some occasions. He's inclined to throw his weight about, and he's got a short fuse. Doesn't take much to rile him."

"What about Nikki Ridley? How did she get on with Rooney?"

"Nikki's got quite a tongue on her. She and Tina Wilson were quite capable of giving Darren as good as they got."

"Ever violent?"

"Not in my lessons, though I had to warn all of them about their language on occasions."

"Where does Simeon Parks fit into all of this?"

"Rather weak character, regarded as a bit of a joke by the rest of the class, and even by Darren's lot he hangs around with."

"Does he have it in for you?"

"Who, Simeon?" Carberry said with surprise. "He's no reason to. I don't pick on him or try to make fun at his expense." Carberry considered the question again, "Is he the one who has made these allegations against me?"

Carberry took the inspector's silence as affirmation. "I don't understand why he'd say that."

"Neither do I, but I think the lad's got some more explaining to do."

"Am I free to leave now?"

"Certainly. Though I'd prefer if you didn't go shooting off to Wales again for a while. We may need to talk to you again."

Mrs Parks was not happy to see the police at her door again. "Why can't you leave him alone! He's not done anything!"

"I'm afraid that's not quite true, Mrs Parks. He's already admitted a serious sexual assault on a young girl."

"But he didn't hurt her!"

"Please, Mrs Parks. We need to speak to Simeon again. Either here or at the police station." D.I. Robbins insisted.

"He's not going to the police station!"

"Mrs Parks, is Simeon here?"

She opened her mouth to launch another tirade about police harassment, then thought better of it. "Yes," she grunted.

"Please ask him to join us. You of course have the right to remain present."

"Hmph!"

Simeon's scars made him look as if he'd been auditioning for a horror movie. He sidled in nervously and sat down.

"Simeon, when we last met, you told me that you had seen Mr Carberry push Nikki to the ground."

"That's right, he did. He did!"

"I'm afraid that not true," said the inspector, "Mr Carberry left for Wales after school on Friday. We have checked his story. It would have been impossible for him to be on the school premises that evening."

Simeon couldn't meet their eyes.

"So, tell us now what really happened."

Simeon cowered, hunching himself up in the chair, and looked at his mother for support.

"You must tell them the truth," she said.

"Did you push Nikki over?"

"No! It was someone else!"

"Who?"

"I...I don't know."

"Don't know or won't tell?" D.I. Robbins pressed him.

"I'm not saying anything else!" Simeon pushed the chair back and ran out of the room.

"Simeon!" his mother called after him.

"What do you think, boss? Is young Parks still lying?"

D.I. Robbins glanced at his sergeant who was driving them back to the station. "I don't know. He still claims someone else pushed the girl to the ground first. And we know it wasn't the teacher."

"Who else could it have been, then? Everyone else is accounted for."

"I wonder. I'd like to have another word with those three lads who found her. And the girl herself. She might remember something."

"How are you feeling now? No headaches?" asked the WPC.

"I'm ok," said Nikki.

"I'm sorry to have to take you back to that evening, but can you remember anything at all about who assaulted you?"

"No, I'm sorry."

"Someone grabbed your arm and you fell?"

"Yes, I think so."

"Not pushed?"

"I don't know, I don't remember."

"And you have no idea who it was?" D.I. Robbins took over.

"No, I didn't see him."

"You're sure it was a him? Could it have been a girl?"

"I...er...I dunno. Haven't really thought about it."

"Lizzie perhaps?"

"Oh you must be joking! I'd have known if it was Mouse!"

"Darren then? He'd grabbed you earlier, so I'm told."

"I'm sorry, I really don't know who it was." Nikki thought for a moment then added, "He had a go a Tina, though."

D.I. Robbins perked up, "When was this?"

"The other week, on the way home from school. Darren, Steve and Sim."

"Was she hurt?"

"Not as much as Sim and Steve. Kneed his balls and got away."

"Did she report it to anyone? Teachers?"

"No, only to me. He threatened her again but she fooled him into thinking she'd got the whole incident recorded on her mobile, and said she'd let everybody have a copy if he tried anything again," Nikki laughed. "Really stuffed him!"

"Thank you for letting us talk to Nikki, Mrs Ridley,"

"This won't take very long, Mr Anson, if we could have a few minutes with Tom." D.I. Robbins said when his knock on the front door was answered. "In your presence, of course," he added.

"Tom! Can you come down!" his father called back into the house, and then invited the detective and the WPC inside.

"Now, Tom," D.I. Robbins began when they were all seated in the lounge, "Cast your mind back carefully to the evening of the disco. You went outside with Steve and Darren for a, ah, breath of fresh air, I understand."

Tom nodded.

"And were the three of you together all the time?"

"Yes, well more or less. Darren had to go for a leak."

"And you then heard the scream? How long had Darren been gone?"

"Yes, after he'd left. I dunno, less than a minute, I guess."

"Could it have been longer? Two minutes? Five minutes perhaps?"

"No, not five, definitely. It didn't seem very long. Two minutes would be stretching it, I think."

"And then what happened?"

"Steve and I started running to where we thought the scream had come from."

"And Darren?"

"He joined us before we found Nikki."

"What direction did he come from?"

"What do you mean?" Tom furrowed his eyebrows, "You're not suggesting that Darren…"

"Did he come towards you, from the side, or catch you up from behind? Think, Tom, this is very important."

"I don't want to get Darren in trouble."

"You won't. Just tell us the truth. We already know that Simeon assaulted Nikki when she was on the ground. But he denies causing her to fall."

Tom thought for a moment. "To be honest I'm not sure. He certainly wasn't coming towards us though."

"And you were all together when you found Nikki?"

"That's right."

"Okay, thanks very much for your help. We've already talked to Steve, by the way."

"Those two lads, their stories seem pretty consistent, sir," the WPC commented as they drove away.

"Yes, I wouldn't mind betting that Rooney was involved, but there's absolutely no proof. However, I'd like to see what he has to say for himself again."

"Is this really necessary, Inspector?" Dr Hallam was very annoyed at a further intrusion, though he did his best to hide his feelings. He thought he'd seen the end of a police presence at the school, particularly as he'd ensured that the injured students had remained at home for a week.

"I apologise for the inconvenience," said D.I. Robbins, "but there are some inconsistencies that we need to clear up."

"I'm afraid Mr Carberry is no longer here."

"We don't need to speak to him again. We are satisfied he was not involved in any of the events on the evening of the disco."

"But…but…that's preposterous! He deliberately…"

"Dr Hallam, whatever internal action you may take over Martyn Carberry is of no concern to us," the inspector interrupted brusquely. "We wish to talk to Darren Rooney again, with your School Counsellor present. Now, if you please."

"Very well, if you must."

"Darren, we need to check some things in your earlier statement." D.I. Robbins began. "You said that you were with Steve and Tom the whole time you were outside."

"Yes, I was."

"But that's not quite true, is it? Your friends have both, independently, told me that you left them to go to the toilet."

"Well, yes, I did, but I only went behind the shed."

"Really? Isn't it more likely that you went off to confront Nikki?"

"That's bloody ridiculous!" Darren shouted, "F'Christ sake, I didn't even know she'd left the hall!"

"Darren, calm down," said Tony Stanford.

"Sorry, sir." Darren took a deep breath. "Look, if I'd have seen her coming out then so would Tom and Steve. Have you asked them?"

A valid point, Tony thought. It appeared that the inspector was also giving the comment some consideration.

"So the first you saw of Nikki was when you found her lying on the ground?"

"Yes, though Tom saw her first. They were already running. I caught up with them."

"And did you tried to help her even though you'd earlier been at loggerheads?"

"Any fool could see she was badly hurt."

"Not such a gallant knight with Tina, were you?"

"What do you mean?"

"You and your friends attacked her on the way home from school, I'm told."

Darren blinked. "Yeah, well. We weren't gonna hurt her. Bitch ran away."

MISSION
STATEMENT

Gentlemen, you now have in writing the complete account of the background and development of my project. I would remind you that it had the full backing of the Headmaster when I first put it forward, and he expressed no concern after personally observing a session in progress.

I admit that my space simulation project was ambitious. I was aware that some issues would generate heated debate and strong opinions, and I exercised some discretion in the use of bad language accordingly. I firmly believed that all the students participating in the exercise had the necessary maturity to contain their emotions within the classroom.

I was devastated to learn that a young student had taken her own life. I regret, too, that other students were injured during the evening of the school disco. The Headmaster, and, may I add, the media have sought to hold me responsible for these tragic events. I have already been exonerated from any blame by the police. I trust that this disciplinary committee will also clear me of all charges of professional misconduct.

Yours respectfully,
Martyn Carberry.

PIONEERS: REPRISE

The students of 10Fleming had been left stunned by the Headmaster's declaration at Friday morning registration.

"He can't do that, can he?" said Tina, as soon as he had left. "He can't stop us going to Lizzie's funeral?"

"Well, stuff him! I'm going anyway." Nikki said forcefully. "She probably saved my life."

"And your virtue," said Patsy.

"Yeah, that too!"

"And it's not fair on Carbunkle! It's not his fault that Sim was such a prat," said Tina. "I was actually beginning to see the purpose of this spaceship thing. I think we should just carry on with the discussions or debriefings, as he called them, in the remaining lessons."

"What, defy the Head's ban?"

"Yeah, Nikki, if you're up for it. Do it for Lizzie and Carbunkle."

Tony Stanford invited the deputation from 10Fleming into his office. Though he had expected to offer some counselling to the students so closely involved in the traumatic events of the past week, he was taken back by their determination.

"You are all agreed about what you want to do?"

"Yes sir," said Roger, "It's a whole class decision."

"Even Darren?"

"Yes, he's on board too. He has Lizzie's diary to thank for letting him off the hook for the assault."

"Well, as regards the funeral, I share your feelings. I will be attending on behalf of the staff. I will have a word with Dr Hallam without mentioning this meeting. While I can't advise you to defy his instructions, I feel that you should follow your conscience and do as you feel appropriate. I can't see that there would be any repercussions."

Stanford looked at their list of demands.

"I'm afraid I can't do anything about the re-instatement of Mr Carberry. The enquiry must take its course. But I think it is highly unlikely that he will return to this school whatever the outcome."

"But he wasn't responsible for what happened to me!"

"I know, Nikki, but there are some, including the Headmaster, who believe that without his project, the terrible events of that disco night would not have happened."

"Does it mean that we can't do any follow up discussions in the lessons either?" said Patsy.

"Hmm, that's more tricky. Again I can't give you carte blanche to ignore the Headmaster. However," Tony Stanford thought for a moment, choosing his words carefully, "your next Current Affairs is today, right?"

"Yes, a double period." said Roger.

"Well, you'll have a supply teacher. It's unlikely she will have been informed about the nature of Mr Carberry's absence or of the Head's edict. Supply teachers usually expect some work to have been left for them to supervise. You could tell her that the work has already been set and you know what to do. If you are all on your best behaviour – no fighting, swearing, and such like – then you could well manage to achieve your aims."

"Thank you, Sir."

Patsy held back as the others left the office. "One personal request, if I may, Mr Stanford. I'd like to let Mr Carberry know that we are following his project through. Would you be able to forward a letter to him? I don't mind if you want to read it through first."

"I think I could do that. I'm sure he would appreciate it."

AFTERMATH

These last two months have been hell.

I would have liked to have gone to Lizzie's funeral but it was made clear I would not be welcome.

The press were pretty scathing, accusing me of encouraging anarchy in the classroom, and many other less pleasant and outrageous activities. I stopped looking at emails and cancelled my Facebook and Twitter accounts. I was banned from contacting former colleagues at school, though Bob stood by me, and, at great personal risk, clandestinely kept me up to date with developments. I was very touched to hear that the whole class supported Patsy's demand that discussion of the social issues raised during the out-of-this-world experience should be allowed to continue in the allotted lesson time. In effect, she facilitated the debriefing I would dearly have loved to undertake myself.

Darren was suspected by the police of being responsible for the initial assault on Nikki since he had a motive, and, it transpired, a possible opportunity, since he had not been in the company of his friends all the time. Nikki herself was unable to identify her attacker.

Simeon was initially charged with assault and attempted rape, but, because of his age and the injuries he'd received, transfer to another school was the only penalty he suffered. And that probably was in his best interest anyway.

Though I was interviewed by the police, they soon concluded that there was nothing for which I could be prosecuted. Much to the Headmaster's displeasure, the disciplinary committee have now cleared me of any wrong doing. Whether or not the letter of support for me signed by all of 10Fleming had any influence on their decision I can only speculate, but I feel a genuine sadness that I won't see that spirited group of youngsters again. However, I have no intention of returning to that school, even if it were possible.

I'm not sure I shall even remain in teaching. Perhaps I'll turn my hand to writing science fiction or computer games.

AUTHOR'S NOTE

Both stories in this book are fiction. All the characters are fictitious and no reference to any person, living or dead, is intended. The dialogue and the course of events are entirely a figment of my imagination.

The basic concept of the Spaceship Earth simulation is, however, fact. During my teaching career in the late 1970s and early 1980s I became involved with a 'Teaching For A World Of Limited Natural Resources' project in Devon. Each of the four pilot secondary schools was encouraged to produce their own teaching module. My contribition, 'Out Of This World' (OOTW) grew as a cross-curricular environmental studies simulation much along the lines of that described in this novel. Students were required to imagine themselves on a voyage of discovery to a new earth-like planet, Terra Nostra where they would establish new independent colonies, each with its own laws and customs, and eventually interact and trade with each other, all, in its original form, within a 12-week module of two hours a week.

I was fortunate enough to be granted a year's sabbattical to further develop and trial the material in other parts of the country and with other age groups, under the auspices of the Centre for Global Education at the University of York. The material was published, in limited edition, within the Devon Education Service and found its way into a number of schools across the country, and also to the Channel Islands, Paris and, I believe, to Milwaukee. By the time I returned to the classroom, however, the introduction of the National Curriculum was stifling innovation and replacing creativity with a tick-box culture. There was no longer any place in the timetable for anything that cut across traditional subject boundaries.

Only now is the wheel beginning to turn full circle with the establishment of academies outside local education authority control and some relaxation of rigid national curriculum. There may once more be a niche for cross-curricular initiatives. With relatively little amendement of the original, all the OOTW material is available on my website, www.out-of-this-world.co.uk for free download. Some areas may still require updating, particularly with reference to the vast volumes of environmental information now available on the internet.

When I was developing the OOTW project, the use of computers in schools was very much in its infancy and the state of the art personal computers were the Sinclair ZX and BBC Master. I did write a very basic monitoring programme for the latter, to accompany the 'space journey' simulation, operated by spaceships magnetically attached to a white screen onto which was projected a scrolling space map. My inspiration for this was an old Waddington's board game called Astron, which I still have in my possession.

'Out Of This World' is set more or less in the present day. The computer simulation described is probably quite feasible now, but it would have been far outside the memory capacity of those early computers, let alone my programming capability then or now.

I should like to thank Mecki Testroet for carrying out a

detailed proof read of the manuscript. I take full responsibility for any remaining errors. I should also like to thank the team at Troubador for getting this, my second novel published by them, into print.

Finally, I should like to dedicate this book to the memory of my former colleague, Alan Keylock, whose support and active participation was instrumental in delivering the environmental education project in the classroom.

Colin Andrews
   March 2015